Praise for Wiss Auguste's
THE ILLUSIONS OF HOPE

"A woman wakes up in the middle of nowhere, her mind a blank slate. What is the life of a woman like? How does she create her own reality? How does she form relationships? How does she interact with other women and with men when she has no memories of who she used to be? *Like Ripples on a Lake* is a powerful feminist tale of the fragilities and the strengths of womankind. It's a rare look at what womanhood can be like." - **Kelly Reed**, Copy Editor, Red Adept Editing

"A young woman wakes up alone and with no idea who she is. She embarks on a journey of creating a new identity but is forced to fight against cruelty and the patriarchy at every turn, even from people she never would have expected." -**Susannah Driver,** Proofreader, Red Adept Editing

From the Pages of
THE ILLUSIONS OF HOPE

"Once again, she felt free. Once again, she found peace. It was music that freed her soul from the dungeon of her mind, and her body responded in kind." **P. 49**

"There's nothing more poisonous to a community than rumors and gossips. They taint the good character of those who effortlessly stand out. They provide mediocre individuals with a mean to become relevant. They set in like gangrene and eat away at the sense of decency that differentiates humans from animals." **P. 52**

"She started to question the real reason behind all this negativity being thrown her way. She was flabbergasted by the backward thinking of humankind. The damaging double standards that fueled gender disparity infuriated her." **P.79**

"Self-confidence is notoriously fickle when it is defined by factors beyond one's control." **P. 81**

"I am trapped in a skin that isn't mine, with a name that isn't mine, playing a role that is no longer mine to play." **P.82**

"She was able to tend to her emotional wounds and patch up her mutilated confidence. She reaffirmed her strength and denied self-doubt the opportunity to fester." **P. 84**

"When it comes to matters of the heart, there are no quadrants or formulas that can be used to measure the truthfulness of words and actions. It is a gamble, an educated guess at best." **P. 202**

THE ILLUSIONS
OF
HOPE

Dear Susan,

Wishing you abundant joy and much success in your future endeavors.

Best Regards,

Wiss A.

Sentinel
Creations Press

Published by: Sentinel Creations Press
New York, NY
www.sentinelcreationspress.com

This book is dedicated to you. May you find the strength to break free from the shackles of archaic and constraining societal expectations. May you always strive to be the person you want to be, not the person they paint you as.

CHAPTER I

***

Her inert body, halfway covered by sand, lay on the ground. A nest of scorpions began to feast on birds' carcasses fifty feet away from her. A light breeze swept a flurry of sand up into her nose and down her throat. She sneezed and coughed repeatedly; the scorpions scattered. She opened her eyes and gaped at her dry hands in disbelief. The sight of her chapped skin freaked her out. The blank stare in her eyes drifted around as she touched her lips then her face. The punishing rays of the sun seared her oddly pale visage. She tried to lean on her arms to get up, but they succumbed to her body weight, causing her to fall on her face. Her unnaturally protruding cheekbones hit the ground first. She turned onto her back and wiped the sand off her face and mouth. She lay there for a little while and tried to gather her senses.

Despite her dull, peeling skin, she was a wealth of beauty. The look in her tired eyes, although confused, was still subtly imposing. The sand added a certain glamour to her hair. It created dreadlock-like tresses that dropped over her temples. She would have made a jealous woman out of Venus herself.

She looked around one last time, but nothing seemed familiar. She was surrounded by an ocean of dunes. It did not take long for her to start feeling hollow minded. It was as if someone had rebooted her brain. She was deprived of the slightest hint of memory. The more she tried to remember, the more her headache intensified. "Why would someone ever want to come to such a dry, uninviting place? Why did I come here?" she asked herself, shuddering and breathing heavily. An intense cramping feeling gripped her lower stomach as she rolled onto her side. The befuddled look on her face testified to the fright brewing inside of her. She was too weak to scream, but even if she did scream, there was no one around to come rescue her. This was not a Disney fairy tale; there was no Prince Charming in sight. It was her reality—it was her life. She gasped for a cup of fresh air and immediately began to cough. There was an abhorrent mixture of smells in the air. She hopelessly looked for shade to shield herself from the grueling sun. Her disappointed eyes met with antagonistic-looking cacti and leafless acacia trees. The desert was a prison without bars; her fears were her shackles.

She crawled to the nearest acacia tree and held onto it to get up. Once again, she scrutinized the horizon for a familiar landmark. Nothing looked familiar, not even the bald palm trees scattered on the very edge of the dunes. Her environment inspired fear, sadness, and desolation. The naked branches of acacias creepily danced to the cadence of the northern breeze. She inhaled the lingering sorrow with every breath she took. As the sun approached its peak, she wrapped her hair up in a ponytail, gathered all her strength, and walked east. Her legs were heavy. A grunt followed each step she took. Each step she took sent a painful sensation up her spine. Each step she took caused her knees to wobble. Yet she walked. She walked aimlessly into the emptiness of the desert. She languished for a couple of hours. As she was beginning to lose hope, she noticed on the horizon what appeared to be a body of water. She could not believe her eyes. A large lake surrounded by a wide variety of tall, healthy trees sat in the middle of the desert. Was her mind playing tricks on her? Was it all a product of her imagination? She feared that her mind was forcing her to see what she desired and needed the most. Like a hasty kitten running to her mother for protection, she ran to the water. Greenery paved her steps as she got closer and closer to the lake. It was not a mirage after all.

The air became more breathable. She reached the lake in no time. She dropped onto her knees and gulped down as much water as humanly possible. A sigh of relief escaped her mouth as she got back up and gazed at the lake. The water was exceptionally clear. There were exotic-looking stones sitting at the bottom of the lake. They mirrored the streams of sunlight and created a kaleidoscopic glimmer over the surface. A few harmless rainbow fish swam swiftly back and forth. They were either playing, mating, or playing with their mates. One or two oversized goldfish sporadically leaped out of the water and performed a series of complex somersaults. It was a welcoming dance for their unexpected guest. She was not going to wait for a more obvious invitation. She quickly removed her clothes and walked into the water until she was neck deep. Her pores embraced the freshness of the water. Her muscles loosened up. Blood restarted flowing intensely through her veins. She started to regain control over her thoughts. Again, she tried to remember her past. Again, she felt hollow minded. "Maybe it is better not to remember," she thought to herself. Why chase foggy memories of heartbreaks? Why dwell on the irreversible? Everything around her was perfect. Everything was in harmony. She was as pure as an infant out of her mother's womb. Her mind was beautiful. Blank, but beautiful. She was the only one capable of truly enjoying the beauty by which she was surrounded. Her perception of joy was unaltered by the strain of societal norms. She was free to like or dislike whatever she deemed likable or dislikeable. Her naked mind wandered as she gently rubbed sand and dead skin off her body. The purity of her soul was shown in the way she touched the surface of the lake and the gentleness with which she allowed nature to take over her body. Her inability to recall past events did not bother her much. She was too overwhelmed by the influx of new, pleasant feelings to worry about her past. Her virgin mind was creating new memories worth holding onto. She peacefully enjoyed the affluent new sensations. She enjoyed the northern breeze caressing her skin and whispering in her ears. She enjoyed the glamorous contrast between the deep-blue lake and the rose-colored sun slowly sliding behind the horizon. She was amused by the way the clouds played hide-and-seek with streams of the dying sun. Her senses were synchronized with Mother Nature, and she felt free. She was too lost in her thoughts to realize that it was going to get dark. The sun sank behind the clouds, and nightfall broke her reverie.

She walked out of the water in a careless fashion, revealing her purity in her nudity. She leaned forward to grab her clothes from the ground. She shook her skirt to get rid of the flurry of sand that had accumulated on top of it. A pair of pockets caught her attention. She hoped to find something in her pockets that would help her make sense of her situation—a piece of paper or some form of identification. What she had hoped to find remains a mystery, but as she pulled out her empty hands from her pockets, her face flushed. The inner corners of her eyebrows rose slightly. She tried to hide her dissatisfaction, but it was impossible to disguise the betraying frown. She needed hope, a sign, something to hold onto. She got nothing. She looked at the lake one last time in an attempt to convince herself that she did not have to leave. Yet, even the nicest places on earth become boring in due course. The greatest moments become dull and tedious once the flame of excitement ceases to burn. Her mind started to wander. Her pressing curiosity began to feed her imagination. What was waiting for her beyond this mountainous desert? The only way to answer this question was to take a leap of faith. She decided to venture into uncharted territories, leaving behind the only thing that had provided her with a sense of comfort, the lake.

She used leaves and bark from a palm tree to craft a flask. It was large enough to hold adequate water for the journey ahead, yet light enough not to be a burden to her delicate shoulders. Her sense of ingenuity was impressive, to say the least. The complexity of the design made it impossible to describe her flask. It sat elegantly on her shoulder and across her back, adding character to her already imposing personality. She resembled one of those nifty explorers on a quest to find the Gemini of the East—or the Holy Grail.

With no memory of her past, no prospect of her fate, she embarked on a journey to nowhere. Her worst enemy was doubt, but she wouldn't allow uncertainty to slow her down. She must have walked for over three hours when she decided to turn around and look back at the distance covered. The lake was no longer visible. She could barely discern the shadows of the trees that had stood so grandly over the water. She knew then that there was no going back, so she pushed forward. The stress of the travel started to take a toll on her. Her legs got weaker by the minute. She licked her dry lips and tasted the saltiness of her sweat mixed with dust. To add insult to injury, she was alarmingly running out of water. She started to question her decision to venture out. In her mind, she was as strong as ever, but her body did not miss an opportunity to remind her that she was not invincible. Her blistered hands became shaky and unsure as she tried to grab her flask. It felt as if the ground was crumbling underneath her bare feet. It freaked her out. The polygonal and uneven patterns of the desiccated mud caused her to stumble a few times. She got back up every time, religiously walking toward nowhere.

First lesson of life: nature is treacherous. Nature was toying with her, and she knew it. The welcoming and cheerful atmosphere around the lake contrasted with the dreadful obstacles that were now being thrown at her. She realized that nature was both welcoming and punishing. Nature was sweet and bitter, like an unending love affair. Nature was callous, unaware of her needs and her wants, her desires and her wishes. The rainbow she'd once admired was now laughing at her. The warm and caressing sun had abandoned her. Water, in which she had bathed neck deep, had now become a rare commodity. The northern breeze that earlier had sneaked so calmly through her curly hair now turned into a gushing, tornadolike wind. She no longer felt safe. It was clear that nature was no longer an ally; danger loomed with every step she took. Nature was a cruel mistress, lashing out at her unforgivingly and taking back the sense of comfort that had once been provided.

She tiptoed her way into the darkness, hoping her weakened legs would not give out. The depth of the darkness surrounding her would have petrified most courageous men and women. Yet she kept walking. She walked aimlessly for hours until she heard a loud humming noise coming toward her. Before she could bat an eye, a blusterous wind wrapped her in a blanket of sand. As she walked toward the Orient, the wind blew ragingly toward the Occident. For every step forward she took, the wind pushed her three steps backward. She fell on her knees, unable to sustain the constant blows of the gushing storm. She was walking into a wall of sand, a wall whose ceiling touched the sky. She desperately screamed for help, but her voice echoed against the façade of a mountain of sand.

Second lesson of life: relief comes when least expected. She waited on her knees until the sandstorm dissipated. The wind whistled away and a sudden calm befell upon her surroundings. She was still temporarily blinded by the sand in her eyes. She panicked. She rubbed her eyes so furiously that she almost scratched her corneas. She eventually managed to get all the sand out of her eyes. A glimmer of hope replaced the fear on her face as she got up and opened her eyes. There was a stream of small lights straight ahead. She was still fairly far, but she saw sporadic clusters of lights spread in the middle of the valley. Yes. There was a small town sitting on the outskirts of the desert. She was sure of it. The simple thought of being able to address another human being motivated her tenfold. She was no longer bothered by the crippling wounds on her feet. She doubled her speed and rushed toward the lights. She had so many questions that she needed answered. She failed to realize that she lacked answers to all the questions awaiting her. She walked for nearly forty-five minutes. As she entered the village, she heard indistinct voices. Loud music, erratic screams, and laughter emanated from a house ten feet away from her. It was a bizarre churchlike tavern.

CHAPTER II

***

The tavern sat in the middle of nowhere, about three miles east of the rest of the village. It was surrounded by yellow-and-brown fencing that converged to create a walkway leading to the entrance. The dull paint on the doors was peeling off, exposing images of saints from the Old Testament. It didn't take her long to realize that the L-shaped tavern used to be a place of worship. The old cross perched on the edge of the roof offered an antithetical contrast to the activities taking place inside the tavern. The hysterical screams and whistling intensified as she approached the inconspicuous dark-green front door. She knocked on the door a couple of times, but nobody responded. A small crack between the wall and the rotten door hinges caught her attention. She peeped. She saw enough to convince her that the tavern was not an appropriate place for a weakened, defenseless girl like herself. Yet her need for human interaction was more pressing than her need for safety. She slowly pushed the door open and walked in. She hoped that a friendly face would invite her in with a smile, but nobody noticed her presence except a furry beige cat. The cat ran up to her, rubbed its back against her legs, and started licking her toes.

A large crowd of mostly men were drinking and cursing at the center of the tavern. The bar was neatly arranged. The bottles of liquor sitting behind the counter reflected a phantasmagoria of colors as the dimmed lights traveled through them. The chairs and tables were arranged diagonally, providing a clear path for servers and dancers alike. Everything appeared shiny and well kept. In the far-left corner of the room, she saw a group of musicians with banjos and pipes, a true band of happy fellows. She did not understand why so many men would gather in such a weird place until she noticed the youthful and careless young ladies dancing in the back of the room. Their youthfulness was suffocating; they had time on their side, and they knew it. One of them caught her attention. She was wearing a red velvet décolleté with a dark-brown brassiere and a semi see-through skirt that did not go past her knees. She was the heart of the party. She led the group of girls left and right; they looked up to her. The dancers seemed so joyous and free that they reminded her of herself back at the lake. What wouldn't she give to get that sense of freedom back?

She gazed at the dancers for a while, hypnotized at times by their enchanting elegance. She suddenly felt self-conscious. She was filled with foreboding; an unpleasant tingling sensation took over her body. She fought the prickling feeling to look over her shoulder, but her curiosity got the better of her. She turned around and looked up. Her wondering eyes met those of an older woman standing majestically on the upper balcony, sizing her up and staring her down nonchalantly. The older woman had puffy, natural dark hair and a darker shade of lipstick. Her upright posture inspired both fear and respect. Her long sapphire dress and matching pendants glimmered under the lights as her hips moved rhythmically to the music. She was of a rare and matured beauty. The look in her eyes was piercing, deadly. She had one of those smiles that doesn't seem to go away—sarcastic, practiced.

The older woman eventually ceased eye contact. She strolled down the stairs and across the dance floor. She stopped by each table to talk to various groups of people, rubbing heads and patting backs. She danced her way through the crowded room, ordered a few waiters around, then walked to the distraught young woman. She grabbed her by the shoulder and gently walked her to the darkest corner of the room.

"Oh, my Jesus! Sweet love, have you lived through a tornado?" she whispered in a calm and sweet voice. Before the amnesiac young woman voiced any response, the older woman began to fix up her hair. She dusted the sand off her shoulders and patiently untangled her dreadlock-like tresses.

"What brought you to this part of the world, dear? I never forget a face, and your face does not look familiar at all," continued the older woman.

"I walked. I can't remember anything," murmured the amnesiac young woman shamefully. She looked down and tried to avoid eye contact. She knew that was not a satisfying answer, but that was her most honest answer. Luckily, the older woman noticed her embarrassment and jumped to her rescue.

"Well, don't you go and worry now, okay? You have made it this far. Now, you are in good hands," said the woman in a reassuring tone. She further examined the young woman's messy hair and shook her head in disbelief.

"What do they call you?"

"I do not remember my name,"

"It's okay, sweetheart. It is going to be fine. Should we go ahead and give you a name? Would you like to pick a new name?"

"I don't know, ma'am. I am just tired and hungry right now—too hungry to worry about names. I can barely feel my feet," said the young woman.

The older woman moved her into the light and looked at her feet closely. She contrived a "genuine" expression of shock.

"Oh Lord! What happened to you? Someone hurt you?"

"I have been walking for many hours. I woke up in the middle of the desert, walked aimlessly for hours until I ran into this place. You are the first person I have talked to."

"Well, you are God's blessing, my dear. You truly are. Such a gentle soul like yourself! You should never have to endure such cruel misfortune. Let's get some food in your stomach and get you situated. We can worry about your name later," concluded the older woman as she snapped her fingers at two teenage girls sitting by the exit corridor.

The young woman felt reassured. She felt safe and cared for. She was in the company of humans—of women who understood her needs. She was in the company of people capable of being sympathetic to her struggles. She was taken to the back room by two very young girls. They walked her through a corridor that led into a very large kitchen. They sat her on a stool, placed a small table in front of her, and filled her bowl with soup. The invigorating smell of the soup took over the whole kitchen and caressed her nostrils as she brought the bowl up to her lips. She burned herself more than once. She paused from time to time to avoid choking on chunks of vegetables and boiled chicken. After she finished drinking her soup, she was escorted down a dark and sleazy set of stairs by the two girls. Not one word was exchanged between them. The walk seemed longer than it was mainly because she did not know what to expect. Once again, her nagging curiosity toyed with her imagination.

They walked her into a convent-like bathing area. The walls were freshly painted. The fresh aroma of lavender suggested that it had been recently cleaned up. She rushed into the first shower booth she came across. It offered a false sense of privacy as she was relying on a mere curtain to keep unwanted eyes at bay. She was too exhausted to worry about privacy. She turned on the faucet and emitted a profound sound of relief as the lukewarm water hit her skin. That shower booth, for the time being, was her cocoon. She could have stayed there all night long if it weren't for a rapidly approaching ruckus. She opened her curtain and found herself face-to-face with four scantily clad young ladies. They were indifferent and almost unaware of her presence. They stopped laughing when they noticed her. They put on fake smiles as they walked past her into their respective shower booths.

She stood there pensively for a couple of minutes. She overhead them referring to the "new girl." They were talking about her. She knew it. A gentle tap on her right shoulder brought her back to earth. She turned around quickly. The older woman had emerged out of the shadows of the wall and was standing behind her, smiling creepily. She had already changed into a satin nightgown.

"Let's take care of those feet of yours. You need to get some rest. Your feet are not made of steel," said the older woman softly.

The older woman escorted her to a medium-sized bedroom around the corner. The bedroom was fully furnished. A large dresser occupied the right side of the room. There was an old television mounted on the wall, hooked to a small sound system. The wall was covered with various wallpapers of different colors and textures. A queen-sized bed with quilted bedspreads sat grandiosely in the center of the room. A wide array of maquillage products laid out on the dresser added the final touch of perfection.

"Sit, honey. Don't be shy. This bed is yours from now on, and so is the bedroom," said the older woman. She then knelt in front of the bed and placed a vase on the floor, between her knees. She grabbed the young woman's mutilated legs and placed them on her lap. She applied a smelly, viscous ointment on the bruised-up feet and legs.

"Everybody is asking me who is my new girl, and I don't know what to tell them. I do not like to not know what to say to my people. It is my obligation to always know what to tell them. So we are going to call you Hope until you remember your name. What do you think? I am certain you will live up to that name and bring lots of joy to this house, dear," explained the older woman.

Hope? It had a certain sense of nobility attached to it. She liked it. She would have liked any name given to her because what she needed more than a name was a sense of belonging, an identity. Now, all she had to do was develop a personality that embodied the meaning behind her name. She was already looking forward to introducing herself to people. She was no longer deprived of an identity.

"Hope, Hope, Hope," she repeated to herself as the woman continued to clean up her wounded feet. She sounded like a toddler who had just mastered a new word. She had taken her first step toward social conditioning, and she was too excited to realize it. By confining herself to being "Hope," she was no longer free. She had heedlessly opened Pandora's box, and she was oblivious to the precariousness of her situation. Her newly acquired sense of individuality facilitated her adaptation but also made her vulnerable. Hope was fooled by the calm that foreshadowed the storm. She was too caught up in niceties to foresee the raging gale brewing ahead of her.

"Hope sounds great. I like it! What is your name? Are you the owner of this place?" asked Hope timidly.

"Everyone calls me Dee. And yes, dear, this is my heaven on earth. And now, it is yours too," responded Dee.

"I do not know what to say. I am truly grateful. I feel as if this is a dream, and I fear that my awakening might be brutal," complained Hope.

"Dear, as long as you carry yourself well, this is as much your home as it is mine. We look out for our own. We will need to find you a job soon, though. Everyone has to earn their keep, you know."

"Of course. I was also thinking about that. I wouldn't want to be a burden to you. I am willing to help in any way that I can."

"That is wonderful to hear, my dear. I knew from the moment I laid eyes on you that you were going to make our home lively again. Why don't you go on and have some sleep? We will discuss your job in the morning."

"Thank you again, Dee. I know I can never thank you enough. I have a favor to ask. Would you please call me my name before you leave? You would be the first person to use it."

"You are a sweetheart, aren't you? Good night, Hope!"

"Good night, Dee!"

Such a candid conversation between two warm souls! Hope turned around and propped her pillow against the headboard. She liked the warmth and candor of Dee, and she liked her new name. The turn of events was not too bad after all; she no longer remembered her past life, but she was ready to start anew. She was ready to create new memories. She was ready to let her adventurous soul explore all the delights life had to offer. She fell asleep wondering what other pleasant surprises the morning would bring to her doorstep. She slept peacefully throughout the night and throughout most of the day as well. She was awakened a little after noon by the same teenage girls who had fed her the day before.

"Hope," whispered one of the girls in a shy voice. "Hope, Dee wants you. Wake up."

Hope was not familiar with her new name quite yet, so it took her a while to realize that she was not dreaming. She ran to the bathroom to wash up and put on a pinkish dress that the girls had brought her. The dress fitted as if it was custom-made. Dee had guessed her size to perfection. Hope looked at herself in a mirror for the very first time and smiled from ear to ear. She was blossoming like daffodils on early-spring days. Her happiness overflowed. Her smile was genuine, and it bothered the teenage girls.

Their jealousy was understandable. Day in and day out, they delivered nice things to other people and fed off guests' crumbs and leftovers. Hope failed to notice the disdain with which she was being leered at as she made her way to Dee's room. The piercing looks in the girls' eyes were frightening. If dirty looks could kill, Hope would have died of countless stab wounds. Hope knocked on Dee's door a couple of times then slowly pushed it open.

 "Don't be a stranger, dear. Come on in," hollered Dee.

She walked out from the back door and complimented Hope on her dress. A light shade of scarlet spread across Hope's timid cheeks.

"Thanks, Dee. I like it! It makes me feel alive."

"Good to hear, dear. Have a seat. We have plenty to talk about," said Dee. She poured herself a cup of chamomile tea. "Have you decided what you want to do? Do you have any specific set of skills? Cooking, maybe?" inquired Dee.

"I don't think so, Dee. I do not recall anything from my previous life. I don't know if I can cook."

"That's right! You did tell me that. That must have been a terrifying experience. You never told me the details."

"All I remember is waking up in the middle of the desert with no memories of who I am. I ventured out with hope of finding answers, and fate brought me to you."

"That is the Lord's blessing, dear. That is not fate nor luck. Don't worry. Everything will come back to you in due time."

"I would sure hope so. I do appreciate everything you do for me. You are a very kind person."

"Don't mention it, dear," said Dee. "It seems like we are going to have to find you something to do that is not too strenuous. Your poor legs have endured enough already. Standing all day in the kitchen would definitely take a toll on them."

Dee stared at the ceiling for nearly two minutes, whispering to herself. One would think she was attempting to decipher some complex math problem. In a eureka moment, she exclaimed, "I have an idea! Can you sing, dear? Or dance? Or maybe both?"

"I guess I can sing if you want me to. I don't remember any songs; the melodies sound familiar, but the words aren't. I will learn them, though."

"Well, there we have it, dear. If you can't sing, you will dance, then!" she said, patting Hope's back and smiling from ear to ear. "I don't know why I did not think about that sooner. Your elegant legs were made to dance."

"I would enjoy dancing very much. I would have to be taught how to, though. I am so sorry. I am starting to feel more and more useless," said Hope as blobs of sweat trailed around her nose.

"We can teach you everything you need to know about dancing, dear. Our girls will take care of you. Don't you worry, okay?"

"Thanks, Dee. I will not let you down."

Hope had struck gold; dancers were the most liked among Dee's girls. Their needs were always taken care of; their frivolous desires were always satisfied. Hope was grateful for the opportunity. She was determined to remain in Dee's good graces by all means necessary. She had promised Dee not to let her down, and she was willing to do everything in her power to fulfill such a promise. But what if she couldn't? What if Dee's expectations surpassed Hope's ability to deliver? What if she was not equipped with the set of skills that would make her invaluable to Dee? She began to worry. The fear of being inadequate and expendable invaded her mind.

Third lesson of life: Moral norms and societal expectations are complex by nature. Hope had no knowledge or memories of social boundaries. Due to her amnesia, she was free from preconceived moral values imposed by any given society. Yet her excitement died out as soon as Dee left the room. She was no longer ablaze with the prospect of a new life. She was pensive, bothered. Why was she so boggled by the self-imposed challenge of meeting Dee's expectations? Was it because deep inside she knew there had to be boundaries she would not cross to please Dee?

The foreseeable challenge of interacting with the other girls also bothered Hope. She wished to fit in because she did not want to be ostracized. Yet her innermost rebellious soul also wanted to stand out. She refused to be mediocre or average. The complex process of social conditioning would have amazed Hope if only she knew that she was being conditioned. She had only been around humans for a few days, and she had already embroiled herself in one of the most intricate social dilemmas: to stand out or to fit in?

CHAPTER III

Enough about Hope. Who is Dee? Delilah Walters, also known as Dee, was the epitome of a successful woman. She had been through some rough times, but she managed to turn her luck around. Born into a dysfunctional family, she learned to fend for herself at a very young age. Her abusive and careless father loved drunkenness more than he loved fatherhood. His life revolved around drugs and liquor. He passed away when Dee was six years old—overdosed on cocaine. Dee's mother battled a range of mental illnesses from depression to schizophrenia until she committed suicide. Dee was eleven years of age. It is unknown how Dee amassed her money. She purchased the tavern in her mid-twenties, and her business had been booming since. She had a natural instinct for business and investment opportunities. In Dee's eyes, Hope was a hell of an investment: she had no memories, no family, and a burning desire to please. Dee intended to groom Hope and turn her into a golden goose.

It had been a few weeks since Hope had walked into the tavern. She was unbothered by the large amount of hair that had grown on her legs. Yet Dee convinced her that it was unladylike and bad for business.

"You don't want your legs looking like you just crawled out of a cave, dear. I know you are indifferent, but it's not about you. It's about them and what they want. It's about what they find attractive. It's about what they are paying to see. You understand?" Dee explained as she smoothly moved the razor blade up and down Hope's legs.

Dee surmounted various obstacles to get to where she was. The one thing she failed to accomplish was freeing herself from the web of patriarchy. Her business revolved around men, around their needs and desires. She was forced to take into consideration their petty demands. The expression on her face attested to her intolerance for men's narrow-mindedness. She hated being powerless. Her inability to wiggle free from the virtual grasp they had on her business made her feel vulnerable.

Hope was oblivious to it all. Dee found her naive indifference comforting. She enjoyed molding her into the person she wanted her to be. Hope's hair was cut to shoulder length because it was preventing people from seeing her smile and her cleavage. She was also introduced to the intricacy of makeup or "maquillage." Dee taught her how to make her lips look fuller and how to hide her very few freckles.

Hope learned more than makeup techniques and dance moves. She learned that her thin lips were something to be ashamed of. She learned that her freckles were to be hidden, always—legs, shaved, always. They taught her to be self-conscious. Her confidence was the price to pay to meet Dee's standards of beauty. She never complained, not once. In her head, she questioned everything that was being drilled into her. Yet, she wanted to please Dee, so she kept her doubt and worries to herself.

Dee spent weeks molding Hope; she wanted her to be impeccable for her debut. Her dance moves were polished and repolished. Her perceived flaws were masked behind concealers and fake smiles. Hope was eager to go out there and make her mark on the world. She was eager to impress Dee and even more eager to prove herself to the other girls, whom constantly looked down on her.

 For her first dance, she was given an option between an easy ballet routine and a very sensual belly dance. She opted for sensuality. Her night of glory finally came. She stepped onto the dance floor on a busy Saturday night in a sapphire-blue chiffon skirt covered with sequins and earth stones. Her brassiere barely covered her chest, leaving her belly exposed. Her oriental face veil added a sense of mystery to her outfit. Despite her halfway-covered face, confidence could be seen in her smiling eyes. The tavern went quiet as she walked to the center of the dance floor. Drums, violins, and banjos broke that silence with an interpretation of "Yearning" by Raul Ferrando.

Hope became one with the music, transcending the limits of imagination. Her waist embraced each note, each beat. Her legs transported the spectators into a world that only she controlled. Her delicate feet didn't seem to be touching the floor. She was completely unaware of the crowd. She spiraled again and again, possessed by the sound of the drums. Like a snake charmer leading a standing cobra with his pungi, Hope controlled the mind of every man at the tavern. Their eyes religiously followed the motion of her hips. As she closed her eyes and let the drums control her senses, she relived the overwhelming sense of completeness that she had once experienced at the lake. Her amnesia was irrelevant as music made her whole again. Once again, she was free. Once again, she found peace. It was music that freed her soul from the dungeon of her mind, and her body responded in kind.

The music finally stopped. Standing ovations, whistling, clapping—the reactions varied, but they all translated into one thing: Hope had mesmerized the crowd. People shouted at her left and right, trying to get her attention.

"What is your name, new girl? Tell us your name, babe!" they shouted.

She wanted to turn around and scream, "Hope," but she did not. From behind the stage, Dee savored the success of Hope more than Hope herself. She got up on stage quickly and took advantage of the momentum created by Hope. She picked up her light-brown dress to avoid walking on it. A warm wash of light illuminated the stage as Dee walked over to the musicians and grabbed a microphone.

"Ladies and gentlemen, it is with great pride and admiration that I stand before you tonight. I know you did not come here for a speech. I know some of you are still daydreaming about her beautiful legs, but I am only asking for thirty seconds of your time. I wish to formally introduce our new girl to you all. She came to us a few weeks ago, broken and lost. Tonight, she stood in front of you, strong and confident. Please stand up! Every single one of you! Stand up to cheer one last time for the delightful Hope!" said Dee in a towering voice.

The warm introduction and praises were heard by everyone, including Hope. She felt accomplished and appreciated. She smiled triumphantly. Her heart was filled with gratitude. Many performances followed. Dee watched Hope steal the spotlight from the other girls, and she could not help being proud of her. A little healthy competition was always good for business, and Dee knew it. Hope raised the bar and redefined dancing. She teased and taunted the other girls and challenged them to match Hope's determination and drive.

Hope never got used to the standing ovations that followed her performances. She danced five nights a week, and every night felt like her first. Her humble attitude allowed her to remain graceful. Yet despite her humbleness, she was not liked among her peers. With fame came loathing; Hope's harshest critics were usually the ones who lacked what it took to rise up to stardom. Hope became the subject of both admiration and aversion. The antipathy that fellow dancers felt toward her was as suffocating as the excessive attention she got from men at the tavern and around town. She would have preferred not having eyes undressing her constantly, but she did not mind being appreciated and desired. Her kind personality prevented her from turning down the unwanted attention. She often forced a smile at the indecent "compliments" for fear of being labelled rude and obnoxious. She built a bad reputation without knowing it. Her nervous smile was perceived as promiscuity.

Fourth lesson of life: rumors are venomous. There's nothing more poisonous to a community than rumors and gossips. They taint the good character of those who effortlessly stand out. They provide mediocre individuals with means to become relevant. They set in like gangrene and eat away at the sense of decency that differentiates humans from animals. The outrageous rumor of Hope's licentious ways spread at an alarming rate. Talk of her promiscuity spread all over town like an airborne plague caught by a zephyr. But what promiscuity? Just rumors and gossips. In the most remote corner of town, people were aware of the new girl that set the tavern ablaze nightly. She was described as heavy-bottomed and obnoxious by some, thin and frail by others. Everyone had an account of her prowess and her look, even those who had never laid eyes on her. Everyone but she knew about her imaginary mischief and wrongdoings.

Hope was unaware of the reputation she had acquired. She was a busy woman. She danced twice a night, opening and closing the stage. She became Dee's bread and butter. Dee could not have foreknown how successful Hope turned out to be. She did not have any friends; her sole focus was perfecting her craft and pleasing Dee. Her dedication to her work showed in her mastery of dance routines that had never been performed before due to their complexity. Her mentors and choreographers ran out of dance routines to teach; they also ran out of compliments to give. Lastly, they ran out of criticism because there was nothing to criticize. As the choreographers became complacent, Hope's artistic side took over. She obsolesced her mentors and began to create her own dance routines. Her obsession with nature showed in her work. She mimicked to perfection the elegantly coquettish mating dance of the peacock. She floated around the dance floor. She was as calm and poised as the white albatross gliding effortlessly.

Dee's candor gradually eclipsed with time. She appreciated and celebrated Hope's success, yet deep inside, she also felt threatened. She no longer felt relevant. Even her most lavish clients—men she considered friends—ignored her presence when Hope was on stage. For the very first time in her life, she walked unnoticed among her clients. They were always too busy gazing at Hope to notice her presence. They talked at length about Hope's bosom and legs. They talked openly about their eagerness to uncover the mysteries hidden under Hope's skirt. They talked about their addictive craving for her forbidden fruit—tales of fantasies and buried desires. Dee heard it all. She was condemned to hear the same stories of what-ifs every single night, week after week after week.

One Sunday night, Dee grew tired of hearing praises about Hope. She retreated to her bedroom, disconcerted. The feeling of inadequacy was consuming her from within. She slid out of her dress and revealed a couple of gut-wrenching cicatrices on her lower left shoulder. They were a testament to battles she had fought and won. She sat in front of her mirror in a pensive mood. There was no telling what was going through her mind until she grabbed a wet towel and angrily removed her makeup. She had always managed to hide her wrinkles from everyone but herself. She took a closer look at her face and murmured, "Wrinkles should merely indicate where smiles have been."

Beautifully said, Mark Twain. Beautifully said, but not convincing enough to chase away the dark thoughts creeping up on Dee's mind. Her wrinkles were not remnants of smiles. They were a reminder of her troubled past, a reminder of her dark memories and broken soul. They were like a map delineating the hurdles of her circuitous journey. She looked at her face in a disdainful manner. She looked at her face and pictured Hope standing behind her, looming over her in her smothering youthfulness. At that very moment, she realized that everything about Hope disgusted her—the radiant skin, the fanciful legs, the curly hair, even the innocent smile.

CHAPTER IV

***

Dee was confronted with a dilemma. Her most productive girl had awoken the darkest form of sentiment in her heart. She was trapped between her need for Hope's services and the desire to see Hope gone. In the midst of her crisis of jealousy, Dee realized that she had to handle the Hope problem before it got out of hand. She thought about removing Hope from the spotlight. She wanted to send her back to the kitchen and have her wash dishes until her hands fell off. Yet doing so came with a price that Dee was not willing to pay. Her best dancers were unable to generate half of the profit Hope generated on a bad night. Hope was the cornerstone of her business. In twenty-five years of business, profit had never been so high. She had gotten used to the sense of security that Hope provided, and she was not about to let that go. A bad night with Hope was still a great night compared to all the nights before Hope.

Jealousy is a very strong motivator, but for a business-minded woman like Dee, money was an even greater motivator. She cast her pride aside and spent days trying to find a solution that would not cost her a small fortune.

Dee finally reached a consensus with her alter ego. The best way to take Hope off her pedestal was to humiliate her. She had to remind Hope that she was expendable like everyone else. Dee resolved to exhaust Hope beyond measure. She wanted to throw her off her dance routines and make a fool out of her. But how?

After concocting the most devious plan in her deranged mind, she summoned Hope to her bedroom. "Rachel, come here!" she screamed. A frightened and sickly young girl came stumbling into her room. "Rachel, do me a favor and go fetch that girl, Hope. She and I need to have a little friendly chat."
Poor Rachel hurried her little feet, running as fast as humanly possible to Hope's room.

"Hey, Dee. What's up? You sent for me?" said Hope.

"Come in, Hope. Close the door behind you, will you? We would not want our little conversation to reach the wrong ears, would we?"

Hope pulled the door behind her and made sure it was all the way closed. She sensed sarcasm in Dee's voice, and it made her a little nervous. She did not like the tone of the conversation, but she was in no position to dictate terms.

"What is it you wanted to talk about? Did I do something wrong?"

"Oh no, dear. You have been doing marvelously well. Don't look so concerned! I am grateful for the work you have been doing. I actually want to reward you for your work ethic. Wouldn't you like to have more responsibility around here, Hope?" asked Dee.

Hope started blushing. "Of course, Dee. I am already appreciative of the fact that you let me put together my own dance routines, but I feel a little more responsibility would not hurt."

"Wonderful! I knew it. You are a trouper! So from now on, you will also help with serving drinks after your performances. One of our girls is very sick, and the bar is always overwhelmed with orders," concluded Dee.

That was not the kind of responsibility Hope had in mind. It was more like a punishment; Hope could feel it in her gut. She refused to give in to negative thoughts, but she knew she was being indirectly scolded for something. She tried her best to hide her disappointment. She thanked Dee for the "opportunity" and left the room.

Until that moment, Hope never thought of Dee as treacherous. It was now clear that she was being taken advantage of. She went back to her room, flustered. She began to contemplate all the things she could do on her own. She thought about opening her own venue and being her own boss. Things would be so much simpler. She would no longer have to worry about pleasing Dee. She thought long and hard about leaving, but she was loyal to a fault. She refused to betray the woman who took her in and gave her life back to her. She convinced herself that serving drinks was only a temporary situation and vowed not to complain.

Dee wholeheartedly enjoyed the little satisfaction that her small victory brought her. Hope struggled every night with the overwhelming tasks of entertaining and then serving unscrupulous men. She never uttered a word of complaint; the last thing she wanted was for the other girls to pity her. She took pride in working hard for every dollar she made. Dee observed her night after night, but Hope denied her the satisfaction of seeing her fail. Her resilience angered Dee beyond measure. After three weeks, Dee grew impatient and decided to tighten the noose. She gave everyone but Hope the night off on a busy Friday. Still, Hope did not complain.

That night, she finished her first dance earlier than usual and hustled to the back room to change into something more comfortable and less flashy. She served drinks all night long, running back and forth, apologizing for things she had no control over. She was exhausted. As she was going through her last round before the closing of the bar, she spilled a red muscatel on a tall dark-haired man seated by the stairs. Hope apologized right away and offered to replace the drink. She was also willing to use her own money to cover the cost of what appeared to be an expensive white tuxedo shirt. She didn't want Dee to hear of her misstep, so she apologized again and again. If there ever was such a thing as a sincere apology, her apologies were the sincerest. To her great surprise, the man laughed, wiped down his shirt with his handkerchief and said, "That is nothing to worry about, lovely. I am not the type of man to get you in trouble over a little stain."

Hope stood there speechless, befuddled. She did not expect a passive reaction from him; she expected to be yelled at. Hope thanked him and began to walk away. The man stood up with a grunt and placed himself in front of her. He grabbed her by the waist, pulled her toward him, and wrapped his arms around her.

"Are you the type of girl to deny a poor man like myself the pleasure of smelling your perfume?" he said as he kissed her neck and sniffed her hair like a dog in heat. "Should I go talk to Delilah and ask her to teach you some manners?" he added.

"Sir, please. Stop," whispered Hope. "I am begging you. Let me go get you another drink."

"How good is a drink when I am holding the most intoxicating and refreshing thing in this room?" he said as he groped Hope's bosom and kissed her ears. Hope felt his whiskey-stinking breath on her neck. "I am going to scream if you don't stop, sir. I swear it. Just let go of me," said Hope. The man did not seem to care much. He pulled Hope closer and squeezed her against his chest.

"Scream then, love. Scream so Dee could run out and come rescue you," joked the man.

Hope fought to free herself from his grip, to no avail. She wanted to scream, but she knew her scream would be muffled by the loud music. She also did not want to make a scene. She managed to free one hand, grabbed a pint of beer on the table, and threw it in his eyes. He let go just enough for Hope to break free and run into the back alley leading to the kitchen. She was no longer worried about Dee's reaction over the spilled drink. She was confused and needed some sort of comfort. She ran straight into Dee's room without knocking, dropped onto her knees, and started crying and coughing intermittently. She choked on her tears a few times.

"Dee! Dee, help me! I… There is a man by the bar…" said Hope.

Dee interrupted her before she could get her words together. "Calm down and stop crying like a little bitch. There are lots of men by the bar. What is going on?" said Dee in an indifferent tone of voice.

"Dee, I am sorry. Please don't yell. There was this man, right? I spilled wine on him, and he started groping and kissing me. I ran. I did not know what to do, so I came to you," explained Hope.

"Oh. I see! You ran, and you came to me? Very well, then. And what exactly do you expect me to do, Hope? Go out there and scold him? Would you like me to go out there, pull him to the side, and lecture him on the importance of self-worth? Or maybe you would like me to take you in my arms, rub your back, and tell you everything is going to be okay. Is that it?" asked Dee.

"Dee, I don't want to dance tonight. Can I skip? I promise I will make it up to you tomorrow. I don't want to run into him again. Please, Dee," begged Hope.

"Hope, you will dance tonight, and you will do very well, or help me God, I will end you. Do not come crying to me like you are some innocent little girl. This is the real world. Now, stop messing up my floor with your pathetic tears and get out."

"I cannot do this anymore, Dee. Please. I will work in the kitchen tonight or whatever. He frightens me." Hope sobbed.

"I decide who does what around here. I decide who breathes, who shits, and who dies around here. And I have decided that you will dance tonight, tomorrow night, and every night thereafter!" screamed Dee, furious and annoyed. Her voice resonated in the room and echoed down the hallway. Her anger was unjustified and unexpected. Dee's outburst of anger was her way of compensating for a curtailed sense of power and her lack of influence on her clients. She took her frustration out on Hope because that was the only thing to do. She knew she would make a fool out of herself, trying to get her customers to behave like saints.

Hope got up and ran out of the room. As soon as she left the room, Dee locked the door behind her. Dee furiously removed her jewelry and threw it against the wall. One could argue that she was much saddened by what had happened to Hope. As she disappeared behind her shower curtain, she wiped off a stream of tears that had begun to roll down her cheeks. It was almost as if she was forbidden to shed tears; she couldn't afford the luxury of crying. To her, tears were synonymous with weakness, and weakness was a liability in her line of work.

Hope held her head with both hands and cried silently as she ran down the hallway. She looked behind herself to see if she was being followed by Dee. She was not. She only had a few seconds to pull herself together and swallow her ruefulness. Her closing dance was overdue. From the second-floor balcony, she heard people screaming her name and demanding to see her. She entered her room and started to get ready for what was going to be a dance to remember. It took her a little less than thirty minutes to get ready. The tavern went silent when she emerged from behind the burgundy curtain and walked on stage.

Her closing performance was remarkable yet dark. She wore a long dark-purple fitted dress with featherlike decorations on the back. The dress magnificently embraced her body. She rebelliously omitted to wear any makeup, concealers, or lip enhancers. Her hair was wrapped in a ponytail to expose her pinkish cheeks and cute freckles. Her dark lipstick harmonized perfectly with the black beaded lace necklace covering her neck. She brought on stage one of those vintage golden canes, with hieroglyphic characters written all over it.

"Nostalgia," by Hanine El Alam. That was her choice of music for her closing dance. The sound of the violin quieted the room as Hope waltzed up and down the stage with anger in her legs and grace on her face, possessed by the goddess of music. She gracefully held her golden cane, flipping and tossing it in the air with the dexterity of a professional juggler. Her cane was cutting through the air with unimaginable speed. A frightening whooshing sound traversed the room every time she vaulted. Hope was picturing Dee at the receiving end of her cane. Every time she waved the cane in the air, she imagined slamming it against Dee's face.

One thing was certain—Hope was no longer giggling and smiling innocently. Her stoic smile was that of a performer trained to smile. The expression on her face, seen for the first time since she'd arrived at the tavern, was that of a woman scorned. Her anger had been awakened by the contemptuous way in which Dee had dismissed her fears and worries. The piercing look in her eyes read the souls of her spectators and judged them harshly for their wicked ways. Nobody noticed the change in attitude—nobody except Dee, watching from the balcony. She watched from beginning to end. She immediately knew troubled times were to come; she saw the disdain in Hope's

eyes. More importantly, she saw herself in Hope. Her
past flashed in front of her, and all the bad memories
came rushing in—a torrent of heartaches,
misfortunes, and mistreatments. *Hell hath no fury like a
woman scorned.* If anyone had the aptitude to recognize
a woman scorned, it was Dee. She knew she had to be
ready for the unthinkable. She knew she had to do
whatever it took to tame the beast awoken in Hope.
Oh, the egregious things people will do in the face of
desperation—Hope was in for a treat.

Hope woke up the next morning with a mild
headache. She had a burning desire to forget
everything about the night before. She wanted to
forget the stench of that stranger breathing down her
neck. She wanted to forget about his filthy hands
touching her breasts. Unfortunately, nobody gets to
pick and choose what to remember and what to
forget. She had a vivid memory of every single second
she spent trapped in that man's arms. She did not
know how to cope with the feelings of disgust boiling
inside of her. Even more outrageous than her
unfortunate encounter was her conversation with
Dee. She realized that she was on her own. She could
no longer rely on Dee's good nature. She had seen a
side of Dee that she didn't know existed, and it was
scary. She saw her switching from sweet and caring to
cruel and daring in a matter of seconds. She didn't
understand what had triggered that reaction. She
asked herself whether it was still possible to maintain

a good relationship with Dee. Everything was drifting away. She was indebted to Dee, but her dignity had taken a blow.

Sometimes bad things happen to prevent worse things from happening. Life fired a warning shot, and Hope got the message; she needed to get out. She did not know how and when it would happen, but she knew it was now inevitable; she and Dee would have to part ways in the near future. She looked at her clock, and it was almost noon. She was still in bed and had no desire to get up. She was hoping to avoid Dee for as long as possible, but her hopes were short lived. Fifteen minutes into her thoughts, Dee knocked on her door—two to three light knocks, no signs of anger.

"Are we still alive in there? May I come in, Hope?" she said as the doorknob rattled.

Hope jumped off her bed, unsettled. She did not know what to say or what to expect. A sheen of sweat covered every inch of her face. The only reason her hands weren't shaking was because she grabbed onto the headboard of the bed.

"Come in. The door is open," answered Hope nervously.

Dee opened the door halfway and walked in with the brightest smile on her face. "Well, what has gotten into you, dear? You look flushed. Are you unwell?" she said in her best impression of a caring friend. Hope knew there was nothing friendly about this friendly visit, yet she found some sort of relief in the fact that Dee was not screaming at her.

"I am okay, Dee, just a little exhausted from last night's shenanigans, but I will be fine after a cold shower. You needed something?"

"Oh no, dear. Just making sure you are all right. You seemed a bit out of it last night. Is there any cause for concern?"

"I am okay. I just feel under the weather, but I am sure it's nothing."

"Glad to hear it. So, listen, if you are expecting an apology for last night, it is just not going to happen, dearest. Sometimes you have got to learn to deal with things on your own. Last night was necessary to remind you that I am not always going to be there to look after you," explained Dee as she hugged Hope.

"I wasn't expecting an apology. I just can't understand what I did wrong. You called me family, but you don't treat me as such," said Hope.

"What you did wrong was running to Mommy the first time something didn't go your way. If you don't like the way you get treated, you can still go back to your little lake in the middle of the desert. It seems like you have forgotten who gave you everything you have. Is your memory acting up again?" said Dee.

Hope tried very hard not to let her anger control her actions. Dee was provoking her, pushing the right buttons at the right times. She had experienced one of the most troubling things there was to experience. Dee treated her amnesia as though it was another insignificant little hiccup. She wanted to unburden herself of all that buried frustration. She wanted to vomit her resentment in Dee's face. She understood how important she was to Dee's business. She had every intention of using that as leverage. So, she let Dee have it– unabridged.

"If you are coming in here to remind me of what you have done for me, hoping that it will make me feel ashamed, you are going to have to find a better strategy. It seems like your memory is failing you. You must be getting on in years. Do I need to remind you that I have tripled your earnings since I started working for you? Why do you treat me like that? I never gave you any reason to be so cruel toward me. You are all I have got, and you know it," said Hope in an elevated tone. Hope's remarks struck a chord with Dee. Hope must have guessed that Dee was insecure about aging. Dee looked at Hope in disbelief. Her perplexed visage turned crimson.

"This place does not revolve around you, idiot! It was there before you, and it will be there after you. How dare you raise your voice at me?" screamed Dee as she reached for the flower vase lying by the door and threw it against the wall next to Hope. "I built this place from my sweat and tears. It was I, alone, who worked all kinds of paying gigs around town to make this place what it is now. You think you are going to show up one day and have everything handed to you? You think you can come in here and walk around like you own the place? You think you have what it takes to tell me—ME—what I should have and should not have done? I will burn this place down to the ground before I let a low-life bitch with oversized breasts tell me how to run my home. I know your type! You swear you are a good girl. Well, I have news for you, dear. Good girls do not wear sleazy dresses exposing their legs to every man willing to look. Good girls don't expose their bosoms, strutting around like used-car salesmen willing to sell to the highest bidder. Good girls do not parade around town like peacocks in heat. Your ingratitude and hypocrisy are as repelling as your cheap perfume and fake smile. Grow the fuck up," Dee ranted.

Hope stood there, stunned. She realized the extent of Dee's hatred. Dee had opened her eyes to the real world. For the very first time, she was aware of what was being said about her around town. She now understood the dirty looks she was getting from other women. She was speechless in the face of such disgusting accusations. She was tormented because she had no way of proving those assumptions wrong. She also did not understand why people were so cruel and judgmental, so affected by the way others lived their lives. She had been judged and sentenced the moment she entered the tavern. Dee had made up her mind about her the moment she laid eyes on her. The sentiments of sympathy and kindness she was shown on her first days were nothing but a ruse. Dee lured her into joining "the family" so that she could use her. She'd never stood a chance; she was the victim of a long con. Her fate was decided based on outrageous speculations about her past life. And her legs, those same legs that once were referred to as a blessing, were now frowned upon. Her blessing was also her curse; her beauty was her downfall. It was now clear to Hope that Dee had launched a campaign to destroy her. Her confidence took a fatal blow. The same person who'd built her up was now trying to bring her down in the cruelest way possible.

But why did nobody blame the married men who always approached her with degrading, indecent propositions? Why did nobody criticize that man who grabbed her and groped her against her will? She started to question the real reason behind all this negativity being thrown her way. She was flabbergasted by the backward thinking of humankind. The damaging double standards that fueled gender disparity infuriated her. She had now experienced the cruelty of both Mother Nature and humans.

The idea of starting over from scratch frightened her even more. She was not yet prepared for life outside of the tavern. She knew how it felt to be out there all alone, and it was an experience she did not want to relive. She decided to keep her head down until she came up with an exit strategy. She was convinced, though, that the world was a cruel place to be in; both nature and mankind were deceiving and wicked.

CHAPTER V

***

Self-confidence is notoriously fickle when it is defined by factors beyond one's control. Hope learned the hard way that her happiness depended on Dee's validation. She had never felt so lost in her entire existence, not even when she was in the middle of the desert, covered with dirt and sand. She yearned for someone trustworthy, sympathetic, and kind to talk to, but she had no one. The other girls hated her, Dee was furious at her, and all the men at the tavern only wanted one thing from her. She created a utopic refuge in her mind to shield herself from her reality. A dusty notebook lying on top of her armoire caught her attention. She grabbed it, ripped off the few used pages, and began to scribble down her thoughts and worries in the form of a letter.

Hey, old notebook! Why are you covered in dust? They used you, took advantage of you, and then discarded you, haven't they? It's okay. I know how you feel. We have each other now. We can confide in each other. I hope you won't find my venting in poor taste. If you do, I hope you will be kind enough to entertain me nonetheless.

There's no other way to explain my situation, so I am going to be blunt: I am lost. I am trapped in a skin that isn't mine, with a name that isn't mine, playing a role that is no longer mine to play. I woke up this morning thinking that everything was going to be fine. I woke up thinking that I could go back to my daily routine. Reality slapped me in the face, and I can no longer deny that I do not belong here. I know I am not welcome here, but I also know she won't just let me leave. I cannot tell you more about my situation because I myself don't know much of what is happening to me. This is the second time I have come across a place that is welcoming at first then inconceivably cruel. Is that what I am to expect from everything and everyone? I refuse to believe it so. I yearn for closure, and I am tempted to beg for forgiveness. I am tempted to beg for a second chance, but I do not believe that would help my situation. I want to apologize to Dee for offending her, but I don't know what my offense is. I want to stop offending her, but the only way to stop offending would be to die; my very existence seems offensive to her. I am called all sorts of names. My dress style is considered smutty because I show too much skin. She encouraged me to stand out, but as soon as I started to do so, I am denied the opportunity to be myself.

I am truly lost. I don't know what is expected of me, but I cannot just fall on my knees and admit defeat. She wants to break me; she wants me to crawl back to her and be her little marionette. I cannot be that person. I

do not recall a single thing from my past, but I am
certain that I was never a pushover. I have overlooked so
much to please this woman, and it is still not enough for
her. I am afraid that I will have to resort to drastic
measures to remedy my desperate situation.

One could never deny the benefits of keeping a
journal or a diary of sorts. Hope felt an instantaneous
sense of relief as soon as she put down her pen. She
was able to tend to her emotional wounds and patch
up her mutilated confidence. She reaffirmed her
strength and denied self-doubt the opportunity to
fester. She closed the notebook and placed it on her
nightstand. Besieged by doubts but empowered by
hope, Hope shut her heavy-lidded eyes and fell into a
deep slumber.

Hope slept for a few hours. At 9:47 p.m., a cool
breeze slid through her semi-open windows and
gently caressed her uncovered legs. She slowly opened
her eyes, stared at the ceiling for a few seconds, then
jumped off the bed. Her closing dance was in an
hour, and she was totally unprepared. She hid the
notebook deep under her mattress; the last thing she
wanted was for Dee to get her hands on it. From her
third-floor window, she saw a large crowd at the
entrance of the tavern. She could feel sweat beading
on her forehead; butterflies invaded her stomach. She
stared at the crowd for a while and replayed Dee's

voice over and over in her head: *"Good girls don't wear revealing clothes."*

She eventually gathered her wits and managed to get a hold of her nerves. She stepped into the bathtub with her clothes on, turned on the water, and let the lukewarm rivulets wash away her sweat and fear. Five minutes later, Hope stepped out of the shower with a newfound strength. She knew she had no other choice but to go out there and dance. She needed to get in front of the rumors, and the best way to do that was to dance the night away as usual. She needed to let Dee know that she was not broken quite yet.

She wore a light-green side-slit dress for the occasion, a symbol of hope and perseverance. The dress revealed her thighs with each step she took. She was defiantly flirtatious. "No, I will not let you walk all over me and destroy my confidence." That was her message to Dee, her message to herself. That was the statement she made as she stood on the dance floor, tall and gracious. She refused to let those vile assumptions and rumors rob her of her happiness.

Hope quickly became a symbol of resilience. There was a silent revolution brewing inside of her, and all the other girls sensed it. They could see the animosity between Dee and Hope, but more importantly, they could tell that Dee was losing control. They began to understand that they were the core of Dee's business.

The last thing Dee needed was a hot-headed Hope stirring up trouble and giving the other girls funny ideas. She could have overlooked Hope's effrontery for the sake of money, but the only things she valued more than money were respect, power, and control. She knew she was not venerated, and she was okay with that as long as she was feared. That fear began to slowly dissipate due to Hope's defiance. Dee needed to restore order and let everyone know that she was still in charge.

Hope overlooked the importance of the battle she was fighting—she underestimated the opponent she was up against. Dee was not the enemy. The enemy was a system—Hope became a threat to a way of life. Dee was reluctant to change because her ego would not allow someone else to challenge her ideals, habits, and routine. In Dee's eyes, Hope was synonymous with change, a bad-for-business kind of change. Hope had to be tamed by whatever means necessary, be they fair or foul.

Hope went about her days joyfully, oblivious to the peril in which her show of confidence had placed her. That Thursday night was like any other Thursday night. The tavern was mildly busy, and most of the girls were off except Hope. After her dance, she walked past a few plastered gentlemen standing in the hallway.

"What a show you put on tonight, love! Breathtaking!" yelled one short gentleman as he groped his privates and laughed.

"Quite a show indeed. If only she carried such versatility in the bedroom," said another man.

"Thank you, thank you," replied Hope timidly. She knew it was not a genuine compliment, but her kind personality mandated that she acknowledge them. She hastened her steps and acted like she did not see the overtly sexual gazes and lips being bitten.

That was the treatment Hope was subjected to, night in and night out. She had become immune to the bigotry. Most of these men saw in her a glimpse of the excitement they craved, so they allowed their animalistic instincts to prevail. It was pointless to try to make them see reason. They were simply a fragment of a bigger problem. They were a mere manifestation of centuries of nurtured bigotry and idiocy. Their sense of entitlement was about as big as their egos, and their egos were twice the size of their brains. Decency was a foreign concept to them; Hope ignored them all and walked into her room.

She only had minutes to change and go back outside. Dee wanted her to help out at the bar again. She quickly removed her turquoise dress and her makeup. She walked to her closet and looked for something more comfortable to slip into. Loud footsteps and indiscernible whispers approached her door as she skimmed through her wardrobe.

"I can hear you behind my doorstep. Quit being perverts. Run back to your wives now!" she yelled, smirking slightly and shaking her head in disbelief.

The whispers stopped, and a creepy silence followed. Hope waited for the footsteps to walk away, but everything went quiet. Her smirk faded into a worried smile. Spooked by such an unusual silence, she tiptoed cautiously to the door and reached for the latch. Before she got a chance to lock the door, it swung wide open and hit her head. She fell to the floor, semiconscious. Hope came back to her senses a few seconds later. Her heart pounded against her chest wall like a caged lion roaring its way out. She looked at her trembling left arm, and the sight of her pulsating veins frightened her. Three tall and muscular men, followed by a very short and flimsy one, barged into her room and locked the door behind themselves.

"Please, don't hurt me. The money is in my bag, behind the red painting on the wall!" screamed Hope. She placed one hand over her exposed chest, the other between her thighs, and continued to scream. "Everything I have is in there! You can have it all!

Please, please don't hurt me. Take the money and go."

They looked at each other and started laughing diabolically. They had a sadistic laugh that genuinely reflected the darkness in their soul.

"It's not about money. Shut up, you filthy wh—" yelled one of her assailants, the short one. He was vehemently slapped by one of his acolytes before he could finish his sentence.

"Shut your ignorant mouth, Max, before I shut it for you," said the tall, bulky man who slapped him.

"But… you… I… you hit me? What the…" said Max.

"Max! I will slap you again right now if you don't shut it!" insisted the man. Max took a few steps back and looked down at his feet like a beaten dog.

After screaming at Max—spineless Maximilian—the man turned to Hope and stared her down. The look in his eyes was a blend of disdain and compassion. It was almost as if he was sympathetic to her supplication but indifferent to her situation. He was clearly the man in charge; the other men did not even try to defend Maximilian.

"If you can double what we are getting paid to be here, we will be on our way before you know it," said the man to Hope.

Hope could not believe her ears. Who would hire goons to terrorize her? It all started to make sense. These men were strangers—unfamiliar faces, unfamiliar accents. They were thugs, not Dee's typical clients. Surprisingly enough, they did not smell as though they had been drinking—except for Maximilian, of course. Maximilian was a drunk, a clueless drunk, a clueless and brainless drunk—one of those drunks who like to harass young girls to feed an egocentric need for power. Maximilian was a lowlife drunk. Hope ran out of adjectives to describe Maximilian as she looked at him with contempt.

"Who is paying you? How much are they paying you? You know what? It does not even matter. All the money I have is behind the painting. Take it and leave me be," sobbed Hope. She could not believe her ears. For some unfathomable reason, someone had hired goons to terrorize her. Who hated her so much that they had to spend money to see her suffer?

The man walked toward the painting and pulled it off the wall. Hope's purple purse was stuffed inside a rather large hole in the wall. He snatched it and went through the purse with haste, throwing everything that wasn't money onto the floor. Hope watched him pocket all her savings, but she was not upset, surprisingly. She felt relieved. In her mind, she had just bought her safety.

"This is barely half of what we have been paid. Trust me, we will not enjoy this more than you do," he said.

Hope's false sense of relief dissipated quickly. She broke into tears and started screaming for help. She screamed her lungs out. The echo of her voice bounced off the walls and drifted away, lost in the quietness of the deserted hallway.

"Scream as hard as you want. Nobody is coming. Nobody can hear you. The more you scream, the more painful it's going to be," said Max while putting the latch back on the door. He just couldn't shut his mouth, that Maximillian.

Hope was bleeding profusely from her temple. She lay on the floor, defenseless, weakened. She begged to be left alone, but her supplications fell on deaf ears. One of the men placed a towel in her mouth and held her arms while another spread her legs open. Her last act of resistance was to close her eyes and hope it was all a dream. She closed her eyes then. She heard them laughing. She heard pants unbuckling and unzipping. She closed her eyes as tightly as possible, and the world became a blur. She drifted into unconsciousness as they stripped her of her dignity.

CHAPTER VI

***

A large gray jay, in its glorious silvery skirt, flew to Hope's window and pecked at it incessantly. The noise resonated inside of Hope's head; it was almost as if someone were putting a nail into her temple. She opened her eyes slowly and tried to get up from the floor. Her damp petticoat was covered in stains—a mix of urine, blood, and semen. She dragged her feet to the door, cracked it open, and peeped outside. A sense of doom hung over the deserted, dark, and narrow hallway. She quickly closed the door back up and locked it.

She walked slowly into her bathroom. The faucet made a squeaking sound as she turned it on. She stood there with a thousand-yard stare, gazing into the water while the tub overflowed. A stream of cold water ran alongside the bathtub and under her feet; it startled her a bit. She quickly turned off the faucet and sat in the tub. Everything still felt like a dream to her. It was one of those unbridled and recurring nightmares. She replayed everything in her mind again and again. She dwelled on the things she should have done differently. "Maybe if I was not so hell-bent on defying Dee, nothing would have happened to me.

Maybe if I had locked my door. I should not have worn such revealing clothes," whispered Hope, rocking back and forth in the water-filled tub. She grabbed the scrubber and started rubbing her skin furiously. Her inner thighs, stomach, and chest started to bruise. The water stung her bruised-up thighs; the excruciatingly stinging pain forced her to stop scrubbing.

Hope eventually got out of the shower and wrapped herself in a pinkish blanket. She gathered the strength of ten men to drag her armoire and place it behind her door. Never again would she allow someone to come into her room uninvited. She fell asleep at around midnight. She was awoken hours later by loud banging on her door.

"Open this door, Hope. Open this fucking door, or I swear to God I will burn it down and you with it!" screamed a furious Dee. Hope was unfazed by Dee's violent outburst. She ignored the banging and the screaming. She buried her face in her mattress and wished Dee away. Eventually, the banging stopped, and the angry footsteps of Dee walked away.

Hope wanted to forget about her assailants; she tried to think of pleasant memories, but to no avail. Her physical and mental wounds would not let her forget. The sight of her bruised-up thighs sent tears down her cheeks as she attempted to get dressed. She vividly remembered every single detail about that night. She remembered Maximilian's crooked and rotten teeth; she remembered his boss's lazy eye. She knew that she would plunge a knife into their chests without blinking if they were to ever cross her path again. Yet she refused to let a mere desire for revenge be her sole motivation to live. She had to find a way to move past everything and keep pushing forward.

It had now been a few weeks since the incident. Hope rarely stepped outside of her room, and Dee never bothered checking on her. The sight of men sent chills down her spine, and imaginary footsteps followed her everywhere she went. Her sanity was hanging by a thin thread, and she knew it. She tried her best to free her mind and go about her business, but she developed an acute sense of self-preservation. In her mind, danger loomed in every corner. She spent half of her day worrying about her safety. She spent the other half dissociating herself from her situation and her identity.

Meanwhile, life was happening without Hope. It took Dee less than three weeks to replace her. The new girl wasn't as talented as Hope, but her grace and elegance made up for her lack of dancing skills. Her dark mocha skin glimmered under the lights of the tavern, and her wild, frizzy hair became a fashion statement. It was amazingly shocking how quickly people's attention shifted. Hope was no longer the main attraction. As time went by, she started to enjoy being out of the spotlight. She enjoyed walking around unnoticed. It was unclear whether Dee was being sympathetic or simply indifferent—it was unclear whether Dee knew what Hope had been through. Yet she gave Hope all the time and space she needed to cope.

After months of begging Dee for forgiveness and a second chance, Hope was reassigned to the kitchen. She hadn't told anyone about her unfortunate encounter with Maximilian and his goons, but she was still tormented by it. She cried herself to sleep every night and woke up with self-inflicted bruises and cuts every morning. Her face was always pale, her facial expression always livid. Hope was a wreck on the inside, but she hid her sorrow well. She took comfort only in the fact that no one knew what had happened to her. Her relationship with Dee was simply nonexistent. She was useless to Dee, and she knew it. She knew it was only a matter of time before Dee tossed her out to the wolves. She decided to keep her head down and save enough money to get by. She was preparing herself for the day Dee would kick her out.

Sundays were the busiest days at the tavern. The town men started drinking early on Sundays. They needed to escape the torturous sound of their wives' voices reminding them how shitty they were as husbands.

The only thing more irrational than a toddler is a grown man bored out of his mind. As more men gathered at the tavern, the night started to pick up. Orders came flying nonstop, and Hope worked overtime to satisfy everyone's needs. She rushed to serve one last customer before her break. As she squeezed past a group of men standing by the kitchen door, someone groped her breast. Hope froze for a few seconds—it was happening again. That was the first thing that crossed her mind. Her hands shook uncontrollably. She dropped the plate of chicken wings she was holding, ran into the kitchen, and grabbed a knife lying on the counter. She heard footsteps running after her. She was determined not to be despoiled of her dignity a second time. She stood in the middle of the kitchen, panting and pacing back and forth. A short, balding man came stumbling around the corner. His large, very nerdy bifocals made him look harmless. He staggered to his feet and mumbled a few words under his breath. He would have fallen on his face if not for the wall on which he leaned.

"Wow, babe. Come on, now. Put that knife away. Come to Daddy. I will take care of you," he blurted out. The slurred speech gave evidence of his intoxication. There was no talking this guy out of what he was set out to do.

"Step back. I swear I will cut your fucking throat!" screamed Hope as she swung the knife at him, nearly slashing his left cheek. "I will fucking kill you if you take one more step closer." Her eyes were bloodshot, and her voice was as menacing as the double-edged knife she was waving.

"Oh, fierce! She is a tough one, that one, isn't she?" he said, swaying and staggering. "From what I have heard, you were not that tough when Dee's cousins entered your bedroom. I heard you enjoyed it too, so don't play tough with me, baby girl. Is it money you want?" he added. Hope dropped the knife promptly. She was transfixed by a sudden stiffness that gripped her core. She pulled on her stomach as if she were trying to extirpate the sharp pain nibbling her from within. Her legs gradually folded under her as her bowels churned. Her secret was out!

"Who told you that? Who else knows? Everyone knows, right? Everyone knows, of course," she said in the softest of voices. That was probably not the appropriate thing to say. Hope could have lied. She could have denied it all, but her brain short-circuited. She had no control over the words she uttered.

Maybe it was empathy, or maybe it was the liquor wearing off. The bald guy backed out slowly and walked away. He left Hope to her own devices, sitting in the middle of the kitchen floor. A river of sorrow rolled down her flushed cheeks. She was tired of living in the shadow of her fears. She had nurtured self-pity for way too long; she no longer had the strength to save face. Her secret was out. Everyone knew about her misfortune, and no one tried to talk to her. No one approached her to offer help.

She got up, stumbled her way to her bedroom, and locked the door behind her. She knew exactly what she needed to do. She reminisced on her short but authentic moments of happiness near the deserted lake. She longed for that freedom again. She ached for that peaceful ambiance. She longed for the sound of whistling frogs in the middle of the night. She longed for the freeing sensation of the breeze going through her hair. Her mind wandered one last time and grasped her very few good memories.

Hope stopped by the closet and grabbed a double-braided rope. She climbed up on her bed and stood at the very edge, staring life down in a daring fashion. She then tied one end of the rope to one of the ceiling beams and the other around her neck, double knotted. She smiled at the prospect of a better life. She was no longer hurt because she was convinced that things would only get better from this moment on. Death was the only solution to her problems—death was her gateway to heaven. Death was her only escape, so she jumped—one big leap forward, thrusting her body into the air.

CHAPTER VII

***

The rotten beam succumbed to Hope's weight and snapped in half. The thundering blast echoed throughout the entire tavern. She landed on the floor, stunned. As the Haitian saying went, *Nobody dies before the day they are supposed to die*. It was not Hope's day to die, so the heavens denied her entry.

Pressed by their morbid curiosity, a large group of people rushed to Hope's doorstep. The commotion they caused in the hallway resembled that of a horror-movie scene. They stepped on each other and even shoved each other out of the way as they tried to feed their inquisitiveness. The two young errand girls were the last to arrive at Hope's room. They piled up in front of Hope's room. One girl tried to open the door, to no avail. It was locked on the inside. A buildup of impatient frustration manifested among the curious folks.

"Hope! Hope! Are you okay in there?" asked one girl as she rattled the doorknob. Her inquiry was answered by a dreary silence.

"Hope! If you are okay, say something! We heard a loud noise," screamed a second girl.

"All right now. We are coming in, Hope," warned a third girl. The three girls tried to forcibly open the door. Dee stood there quietly and watched them slam their shoulders against the door over and over until the door hinges began to bulge.

"Stop! All of you just fucking stop before you break my door! I have the key!" finally yelled Dee. The girls stepped aside as Dee took her sweet time to open the door.

As soon as the door swung open, everyone rushed in. They encircled Hope sitting on the floor. She had a rope around her neck and debris from the collapsed ceiling all around her. She couldn't help thinking that her whole existence was a failure. She had failed at everything she attempted to do; she had even failed at dying. She looked at the group of people surrounding her, and her eyes were met with Dee's indifference and disgust.

"Back to work, everyone! Now!" screamed Dee before she spat on Hope on the floor and walked away.

Not one person dared to defy Dee; not one person dared to help Hope off the floor. They all scattered like dead leaves at the mercy of strong winds. Hope's room was empty before she blinked an eye. Some will say that they scattered because they feared Dee's wrath. Others will say it was a total lack of compassion. Hope did not care to know the reason behind such inhumane behavior; she had greater concerns.

Without the slightest hint of doubt, she packed up an old suitcase travel with most of her dresses. She hid the little money she had left in her bra and walked out. She could have tried to sneak out through the rear door to avoid confronting Dee. But she didn't. Like a beaten dog with its tail between its legs, Hope walked sluggishly through the kitchen, toward the front door. The tavern fell silent. Everyone stopped whatever they were doing and slowly followed Hope from a distance. The sound of her suitcase scraping the floorboard added a sense of drama to this already nerve-racking moment. Shame conquered Hope's senses and forced her to glue her eyes to the floor.

"Hey, Hope. How are you feeling?" asked a young girl timidly.

"How do you think she is feeling, Claire? Stop asking stupid questions," hurled another half-naked girl.

Claire was a sweet girl. She always kept to herself. Just like Hope, she did not have any friends. She was sincerely troubled by Hope's state of mind, but Hope simply lacked the strength to entertain her concerns.

She lumbered with her suitcase toward the double door that separated the kitchen from the bar.

"Where do you think you are going?" screamed Dee from the second floor's balcony. "You still haven't learned your lesson, have you?"

Hope looked up, moved the lock of hair that was covering her left eye, and smiled. It was not a real smile. It was an angry smile, one of those smiles that says more than words could ever say. She smiled and kept walking, completely ignoring Dee and her empty threats. She was not being defiant. She was not rebelling, nor was she trying to embarrass Dee. She simply no longer feared her. She was no longer compelled to exude self-pity. In fact, she pitied Dee. She saw Dee's flaws. She saw her weaknesses and insecurities hidden beneath that nasty demeanor.

"Hey, filthy whore! I am talking to you," continued Dee as Hope kept walking.

"You and I have nothing to talk about. You will have to kill me today if you want me to stay here. Or maybe you should pay your cousins to rape me again—right here. Right now. In front of everyone," responded Hope in a calm yet somber voice.

Dee stuttered for a few seconds. Hope knew Dee was the mastermind behind the rape. The accusation caught Dee by surprise. She looked around the tavern to gauge the reaction of the silent group of girls who were witnessing the exchange, but they all avoided eye contact. By the time she gathered all her senses, Hope had already walked out of the front door.

"Get back to work!" Dee yelled at her kitchen staff. That anger she had cultivated against Hope needed to be released.

Hope walked aimlessly down the main road for a few hours. She occasionally looked back to make sure Dee was not coming after her. Once again, she was on the road to nowhere; everything felt like déjà vu. She now had a name, and she had memories to rely on—more bad memories than good, but memories nonetheless. She had ninety-seven dollars in her wallet, a heart filled with remorse, and a bleeding soul. She had sacrificed so much to gain everyone's admiration and approval, and all she got in return was ninety-seven dollars and a battered self-esteem. Dee gave her an identity, but her personality was hers to nurture and preserve. She failed to do so. Her financial situation was troublesome, her mental state even more so. Would she ever be able to trust again? Would she ever allow a man to come near her? Would she ever accept the fact that her past did not have to dictate her future? Only time would answer her pressing questions.

Hope cherished her name dearly. In the days to come, that name would be a reminder that people are not to be trusted. It would be a constant reminder of Dee, the dark soul who cast a shadow over her happiness and took her down a path of desperation. She was certain that more troublesome days were to come. She was also equally certain that she would never take kindness at face value. She finally walked out of the town and put as much distance as she could between herself and the tavern.

Hope walked until nightfall. She came across a convent surrounded by gardens and farmhouses. Her legs were cold, and her nose was dripping. Her skepticism wreaked havoc inside her mind, but she needed to rest. She knocked timidly on the door after hiding her suitcase under the bushes. A young nun opened the door. She was no older than nineteen years of age. Happiness blossomed on her face at the sight of Hope.

"Good afternoon. I was wondering if you would let me spend the night here tonight. I have a long way to go, and it is getting really dark and scary out here," explained Hope to the young nun.

"Come on in, my child. We don't have a spare bedroom, but you are always welcome in the house of the Lord," said the nun cheerfully. Hope was at least five years older than the young nun. Being called "my

79

child" would have amused her a bit if her mind were not already so overwhelmed with worries.

"Thank you. I won't be needing a bedroom or bed. Anywhere is fine," said Hope.

Hope entered the convent and was escorted to a room right next to the dormitories. It had only been hours since she swore to never trust anyone, yet she felt a bit comfortable in the house of the Lord. There was something about the nun that made Hope feel comfortable and safe. That clerical collar provided a false sense of safety—false because nuns, like any other human being, are flawed. The nun fixed Hope a makeshift bed on the floor. Hope didn't take long to fall asleep despite her desire to stay awake and vigilant all night long. Her body and mind were exhausted beyond measure.

It was a very cold night with winds blowing north and south, tearing apart branches, and ripping roof tiles off the farmhouses. Yet Hope slept through the night like a newborn infant. Her breathing was soft. In the middle of the night, the young nun got out of bed and checked on Hope. She stood over her for a few seconds. She then placed a comforter over Hope's shivering legs and thighs and went back to bed.

A pair of persistent cuckoos disturbed Hope's dreams with their morning tune. She seemed miffed by the tenacity of her new friends. She was not displeased by their serenade, but she would have rather enjoyed her sleep a little longer. She was annoyed because she was now forced to think about things she wanted to forget. She yawned then tried to stretch her legs. The blanket caught her attention. She appreciated the kindness of the nun; she smiled from ear to ear. A frown quickly replaced that smile as she realized how close a stranger had gotten to her while she was asleep. Once again, her fears overwhelmed her fragile mind. She neatly folded the blanket and placed it near the window. She packed up her things and left without a thank-you or an explanation. She had no way of explaining her fears and concerns to the young nun without being bombarded with questions. It was well known that nuns and priests have a propensity to be inquisitive.

Hope lived on her own for three months. She spent her mornings panhandling on a busy corner of Elm Street and her evenings under a blanket, on the first floor of an abandoned house. She rarely slept at night. How could she? Danger was always imminent; meth addicts had tried to steal her money more times than she could count.

One Tuesday, Hope dozed off during the late hours of the afternoon and woke up to one of the homeless guys sniffing her hair. She jumped and screamed as loudly as she could. The man ran out of the abandoned house, never to come back. That was Hope's wakeup call; her situation was unlivable, and she had to do something about it. The very next afternoon, she took the uptown bus to Main Street to look for a job. By the time she reached her destination, it was already late. Most of the food places had already been closed except for one, *The Concord*. Hope pulled the door open and walked in. There were two waitresses wiping off the tables and sweeping the floor.

"Hello. Good evening. Excuse me," said Hope to the waitresses. One female waitress turned around, but before she could utter a word, a short young man in a gray suit emerged from the back room.

"Out! Out! We are closed! There are no leftovers, and there is nobody here to beg for money. Get out!" screamed the young man. He turned to the waitress and screamed at her as well. "Catherine, I swear to God this is the last time I will tell you to not bring your people in here. I know you left the door open on purpose for her to come in."

"I thought the door was closed, sir. I really did. I don't know her. She is not my people."

"Are you calling me a liar?" said the short young man, raising a glass of water and threatening to throw it on Catherine.

"Enough!" said an older gentleman out of nowhere as he got up from behind the counter. "Catherine, go throw this bag out," he added.

Hope ran outside, ashamed and distraught. She did not even get a chance to inquire about a job. It was already eleven o'clock at night, and she was too frightened to hop on the downtown bus. She walked around the restaurant and noticed a large dumpster in the deserted backyard. She laid a few cardboard boxes on the floor behind the dumpster; that was going to be her bed for the night. As she tried to lie down, the rear door of the restaurant swung open. Hope jumped up and grabbed her hand bag, ready to flee.

"Who's back there?" yelled Catherine.

"Sorry. Sorry. I am leaving. Sorry for getting you yelled at. I don't want to cause you any more trouble," said Hope, emerging from behind the large dumpster.

"Oh, it's you! No, it's no trouble at all. He is always screaming at everyone. Thank God he is not the boss. He only listens to his dad," explained Catherine as she approached the dumpster.

"Yeah, he sounds horrible. I just wanted to apply for a job. I was not trying to ask for food," explained Hope.

"A job? Dressed like that? Girl, who is going to hire you dressed like that? I will tell you who. Nobody. What is your name?" inquired Catherine.

"My name is Hope. You are Catherine, right?"

"Right. And you were doing what exactly behind the dumpster?" asked Catherine, skeptical.

"Nothing. Just sleeping. I am homeless. I usually sleep at a place downtown, but it's too late and too dangerous to take the bus now."

"Wait here. My shift ends in fifteen minutes. We can take the bus down together. I am homeless as well," said Catherine sympathetically.

They took the downtown bus together. Hope did not know it yet, but that was the beginning of a beautiful friendship. They quickly developed an inextricable bond. Homelessness was a beast neither of them wanted to confront alone. In companionship, they found strength and comfort. They confided in each other. They bonded over heartbroken stories and insecurities. Hope vented about her encounter with the filthy Maximilian and his group of goons.

Catherine vented about her uphill battle to overcome a meth addiction.

CHAPTER VIII

***

Hope and Catherine shared a small hut under the Rhapsodic Bridge. It was a modest home that they progressively built out of cardboard boxes and various pieces of wood. The hut was camouflaged under some dark-colored tarps to keep unwanted eyes at bay. The inside was not very spacious, but neither Hope nor Catherine needed a lot of space. All they needed was each other. The hut was large enough to fit a rugged queen-size mattress Catherine had purchased at a thrift shop. Their days were atypical as they didn't know what to expect. Every day was an adventure with their freedom and safety at stake. They played a constant cat-and-mouse game with the Department of Homeless Services, eluding every attempt to place them in a shelter. Shelters were not safe; Hope and Catherine refused to live among thieves and drug users.

Despite the unpredictable nature of their lifestyle, they had routines like everyone else. Catherine would drag Hope to church every Sunday morning. She wanted to give her something to look forward to, she wanted to give her hope for a better tomorrow. Wednesday evenings were dedicated to picnics at the park because that was Catherine's only day off. Thursday mornings were hair day. They usually woke up early to get water from the fire hydrant, wash their hair, and act foolish. Catherine took pleasure in watching Hope laugh. They sometimes played around for hours, throwing water balloons at each other like teenagers. It was refreshing to see Hope embracing life. She slowly regained a certain joie de vivre. Their living conditions were not ideal. The challenges of homelessness were far beyond the realm of one's imagination. Yet they made the best of it, and they were happy. They found happiness not in what they possessed but rather in each other.

One Thursday, Hope woke up at the break of dawn with cramps and stomach pains. She tried to hide her pain, for fear of waking up Catherine, but she could no longer stand the severe aching and spasms. It was as if every muscle in her abdomen was contracting tightly and refused to relax. A grunt eventually escaped her mouth and woke up Catherine.

"Are you all right, Hope?"

"Yeah, I am fine. Just period cramps," she moaned. "They will go away."

"Are you sure, Hope? You look like death, hon."

"I am fine. These cramps just hurt so badly. I haven't had my period in so long. That's probably why."

"We should get you checked out, hon. You don't seem all right. Let's go. I will take you to the clinic."

Hope was reluctant to go to the clinic. She blamed her pain on the amount of stress she had endured in the past couple of months. Catherine would not take no for an answer. Before Hope knew it, she was sitting in a taxi, on her way to the women's clinic. Hope clung to the seat belt as if her life depended on it. Her flushed face was cause for panic.

"It's going to be all right, Hope. We are almost there," said Catherine as she patted Hope's back.

Catherine was as scared as Hope, but she couldn't let her see the fear in her eyes. Catherine knew that all good friendship was built on honesty. Yet honesty was the last thing Hope needed at the moment. It was Catherine's duty to remain strong and reassuring. Hope was not built to handle hard truth, so their friendship warranted the use of a white lie every now and then. These lies helped boost Hope's confidence and strength of character.

Hope had lost all color in her face; a river of sweat trickled down her forehead. She mopped it with her forearms and looked at Catherine in despair. Her eyes begged for help; Catherine grabbed her frigid hand to reassure her. Ten minutes later, the taxi pulled up in front of the clinic.

"Open the door. Let us out, please!" said Catherine to the driver even before the car came to a full stop. She hopped out of the cab and rushed Hope inside as quickly and safely as possible. She grabbed the attention of the first nurse she encountered.

"Can somebody help her? She is in so much pain. I have never seen her like that before," said Catherine in a worried voice. The middle-aged nurse practitioner took one glance at Hope and immediately escorted her into an exam room, apologizing to the other people waiting in line to register.

"Ma'am? Ma'am, can you hear me? How are we feeling today?"

"My stomach is killing me; I can't take it anymore. I am going to die, aren't I?" mumbled Hope with a grunt.

"Nobody is dying today, dear. Rest assured. Any other discomfort besides the sharp pain and the cramps?"

"Not really. No. Just the pain."

"All right then. It doesn't seem to be anything too serious. It could be period cramps, or it could be something you ate last night. We are going to take your vitals then give you a temporary pain killer. We will also run some blood tests just to rule everything out. Don't worry, dear. Sit tight. We will get you out of here in no time," said the nurse practitioner. A little less than half an hour went by before another nurse entered the room. Hope was in and out of sleep due to the pain killer. She was startled by the cold hand placed on her shoulder.

"Apologies, ma'am. I didn't mean to startle you."

"Oh no. It's all right. Your hand was a little cold, that's all."

"My apologies, once again. I am just here to get some blood samples from you, if you don't mind."

"Of course not," said Hope as she extended her forearm. The gentle nurse collected two samples of blood and walked out of the room. Hope stared at the clock impatiently. She was convinced that the doctors had forgotten about her. She could hear them talking and laughing outside. She waited anxiously for hours. As time dragged on, she wished Catherine were by her side. Unfortunately, Catherine had to rush to work. She could not afford to lose her job. Hope dozed off for a bit. It was already dark outside when

Hope woke up from her slumber. A young doctor was right next to her, taking her vitals again.

"Ah! You are up. Perfect! How are we feeling? Sorry for the long wait. We are a little overbooked today."

"I am all right. It's no big deal. What's going on?" inquired Hope.

"Oh, nothing at all, dear. I was just checking your vitals again; your blood pressure was a little low earlier today. So… we have your results, and we have good news. You are a little dehydrated but nothing to worry about. Everything else seems fine. You are in pretty good health, and we are going to help you stay healthy. Try not to stress yourself out too much. It might affect the baby's health."

"The baby. What baby?"

"Oh! You are expecting, hon. I thought you already knew. You are anywhere from twenty-one to twenty-three weeks pregnant. Congratulations!" replied the doctor.

"Pregnant? Pregnant as in there-is-a-baby-inside-of-me pregnant? There must be a mistake! This is impossible! I can't be pregnant! You need to run these tests again, Doctor!" said Hope. She closed her eyes tightly, but tears managed to sneak out. She refused to believe what she had just heard. Her chronicle was unending. The burden of her past was unshakable, no matter how hard she tried.

"The pregnancy test was pretty conclusive, ma'am," said the doctor, confused.

"No, no, no. You are going to go back and run the test again. That is exactly what you are going to do. Then you are going to come back to me and apologize for making such a big mistake," explained Hope in an elevated tone of voice. She was not herself. Her erratic behavior frightened the doctor a bit.

"Ma'am, we ran the test many times. The result is conclusive," whispered the young doctor as if she was trying not to be heard by the little mob of nurses that had formed behind the window.

Hope refused to have a child that was going to remind her of everything she'd hoped to erase from her memory. No! She was not going to have that child! She had made up her mind in a matter of seconds. It wasn't fair to bring a child into this world of sin and debauchery. It wasn't fair to look at a child and see in her innocent little eyes a constant reminder of scumbags like Maximilian. She wouldn't allow herself to jeopardize the happiness of an innocent child. She refused to carry around a token of her misfortune.

A mother's love extends beyond what eyes can see and what minds can comprehend. A mother's love begins before she gives birth. Hope loved her child too much to subject her to such hatred and confusion. She was unprepared to be a mother, and she knew it. So often had she fantasized about true love. So often had she prayed for a life of happiness alongside the man of her dreams. She dreamt of kids running in her backyard. She dreamt of snowball fights in wintertime, of "Welcome home, Daddy!" screams. She refused to live the rest of her life on broken dreams. Hope got up and sat pensively on the edge of the bed. Her mind traveled miles back into her torrid past. Lost in her thoughts, she forgot about the doctor still standing next to her.

"Ma'am? Is there anyone you wish to contact?" said the doctor.

"No. What I wish is to abort this pregnancy. I cannot go through with it."

"Are you sure, ma'am? You should contact the father."

"I said I am fucking fine!" yelled Hope as she threw her cup of water against the wall, spilling most of it on the doctor's blouse. The young doctor immediately understood the complexity of the situation. A sentiment of guilt took her over for mentioning the father.

"We have everything in place to help you every step of the way, ma'am. I can give you some alone time if you wish. I will be right outside the room. If you need anything, let me know."

"I already told you what I need. I do not want to have this child. I need an abortion."

"Okay. Okay. We can talk about that too. Take a minute to think about it, okay? I will be right back." The young doctor rushed out of the room before Hope uttered another word. She walked back in five minutes later, accompanied by an older physician.

"Hello, Hope. My name is Julia, and I am the senior counselor here at the clinic. I am here to make sure you get everything you need."

"Hey, Julia. Here goes a question for you. Why do you guys keep offering me everything I need, but Miss Pocahontas over there keeps ignoring my one and only request? I want to end this fucking pregnancy. That's *all* I need."

"Well, that's actually why I am here, ma'am. The doctor notified me of your desire to abort the pregnancy. Unfortunately, your situation is a little complicated."

"Complicated? Complicated because I can't pay for it? Complicated because I do not fit the profile of your typical client? You have got to be kidding me. Unbelievable."

"Ma'am, money has nothing to do with it. You are twenty-two weeks pregnant, and unfortunately, state law bans abortion after the twenty-week mark. You are in good health, and so is the baby. Unless you were raped, we really cannot make any exception, ma'am. It is out of our hands."

Hope looked shocked and confused. Her mind was entangled; everything stopped making sense. Why did state laws have a say in her decision to procreate or not to procreate? She was the one carrying the child. She was the one who languished in agony with cramps that wouldn't go away. She was the one who would have to deal with possible complications of pregnancy, not some legislator sitting behind an antique oak desk, drinking cheap liquor. She couldn't understand why a group of bigoted men with an ego complex controlled a woman's decision to abort a pregnancy. Were they going to be there every step of the way to provide both moral and financial support?

The idea of having to get permission to end her pregnancy infuriated her beyond measure. The idea of relying on arrogant and self-centered men to decide her future infuriated her even more. She asked herself whether she should open up about her rape so she could get approved for her abortion. Every muscle in her body was against divulging her secret, but if there was one thing she wanted more than keeping her secret, it was the abortion.

"Well, I was raped. I was raped multiple times. I was raped multiple times by multiple men in one night. Does that make things easier for you? Does that qualify me now for a fucking abortion?" blurted Hope in tears. The doctors quickly ceased eye contact with Hope and stared at their feet. They were astounded by her confession. The young doctor tried to talk, but her shaky, halting voice failed her.

"We are so very sorry to hear that, ma'am. We will do the best we can to help you through such an awful experience. It is a hard time, but I can assure you things will only get better from this point on. There are procedures to be followed, but we shouldn't have a problem getting you approved on a rape exception. The only thing we will need from you is a police report," explained the more composed counselor.

Hope did not have a police report. *Back to square one.* Hope had shared her most cherished secret with two strangers who, as far as she was concerned, were indifferent to her situation. She had shared her secret with the hopes of getting an abortion, and it was clear to her now that she was caught up in a mesh of bureaucratic red tape.

"Police report? Are you fucking kidding me? You think my first thought after being savagely raped was to run to the police and tell them every detail about it?"

"We know it's difficult, but that would have been the sound thing to do, ma'am. You've got to alert the authorities," said the counselor. The young doctor was still in a state of disbelief. She could not comment on the matter. Her eyes never left the floor.

"How do you know it is difficult? Have you been raped before? No, I did not think so. So you don't know shit. You don't know how hard it was for me to look at myself in a mirror. You don't know how hard it was for me to walk past a group of men and wonder if it was going to happen again. You don't know how hard it still is to wake up every morning and know that I will never be able to fully trust a man again. I don't have a fucking police report because I was not thinking soundly after being despoiled of my dignity. I am sorry. I am sorry for not doing the sound thing and alerting the fucking authorities. I am alerting you now! So do your job, and stop looking at

97

me like I am a fucking alien with seven horns!" screamed an angered Hope. A large crowd of nurses and patients piled up behind Hope's window. The doctors grew annoyed at Hope's tone.

"Ma'am, we truly understand your frustration, but you are going to have to calm down. This is a medical institution, and the screaming is not conducive to the services we provide here," explained the counselor. Such a subtle warning did not deter Hope. Her mind was working at the speed of light, and her nerves were fired up. There was no stopping her.

"Well, if this a medical facility, then you should not have any problem helping me get the medical procedure that I need. Do you guys have kids? Look me in the eyes and tell me that you would let some law decide the fate of your unborn child if you were in my position. Look me in the eyes and lie to me! Tell me that you would let a bunch of conservative scumbags dictate your choices. No, of course you wouldn't. Yet you allow them to force me to keep a child that I do not wish to keep, a child to whom I have nothing but suffering to offer. You would allow them to force me to keep a child that will come into this world with the blood of rapists and murderers flowing through her veins. Fucking animals. All of them. All of you."

"We are not trying to convince you to carry to term against your will, ma'am. You seem shocked at the moment. Abortion will probably not be what you want when you calm down," explained the counselor, a little annoyed by Hope's cursing.

"It's not about what I want. This is what I need! Don't you dare tell me what I may or may not want, and don't you dare tell me to calm down!" explained Hope while sobbing in her sleeve. "This is a necessity, not a mere desire. My heart aches, and my legs weaken when I think about the joy that a child usually brings to a mother. Yet I know my child would only bring me pain and remorse."

"Ma'am, we understand this is not ideal, but we cannot break the law regardless of how we feel. You are asking us to put our careers on the line."

"My fucking life is on the line! The happiness of a child is on the line! My fucking sanity is on the line, for Christ's sake! You want a more extensive list of things that are on the line? Your dignity as a human being is on the line. You are allowing men to walk all over you, camouflaged behind the Law. Your inaction fuels their egos. They are empowered because people like yourself, people capable of making a stand, decide to stay quiet for the sake of a paycheck. Every time that you deny a woman like myself the right to make key decisions about her body and her health, you empower them. They disguise their true intentions and their greed for power behind a fictitious moral compass. People like you help them keep the lie alive."

"Ma'am, we have other options available to you. While we understand your position, we cannot go ahead and schedule the abortion. Please give us a few minutes, and we will put together a list of options for you. You could also consider neighboring states with lax abortion laws," said the young doctor, touched by Hope's tirade.

"Ignorance spreads like a pestilence. It's a pestilence that has plagued this hospital in its entirety," said Hope as she walked out of the room and out of the clinic. Her fire had burned out. She did not have any money to make it to the next clinic. She couldn't afford to travel to another city, let alone another state. She thought about asking Catherine for help, but Catherine had already done so much. How was she going to break the news to Catherine? How was she going to tell Catherine that her rapists had impregnated her?

CHAPTER IX

***

Traumatizing experiences stay with us forever. Our stories are written within our flesh in indelible ink. Sometimes, we try to bury unwanted memories, but sooner or later, they arise from the abyss in which they've been entombed.

Hope was haunted by much more than memories; she was carrying the offspring of her rapists. She walked out of the clinic and sat on the front steps. Her legs were too weak to go anywhere else. She dug deep inside her pocket and pulled out her phone; her shaky hands made it difficult to dial any number. She struggled with it for a while and eventually placed a phone call to Catherine.

"Cathy, come get me, please," she whispered in a sobbing voice as soon as Catherine picked up the phone.

"Hope? What's going on? I am on my way back to the hospital. I asked to leave work early. What's wrong, baby?"

"Everything, Cathy! Everything is wrong! I am pregnant. What am I going to do?"

"Oh my God! Oh my God! Oh my God, Hope. I am so very sorry. It's going to be okay, baby girl. I will be there with you every step of the way."

"Cathy, I want an abortion. I want an abortion, and they won't let me have one."

"What do you mean, they won't let you? Who won't let you?" said Catherine, raging.

"The hospital. The doctors. They are saying abortion is not legal after twenty weeks. Catherine, you have got to help me. I cannot have this baby."

"We will find a way, Hope. I am coming to get you right now. We will find a way. I promise."

Catherine took a taxi to the hospital and took Hope home safely. Over the following weeks, they tried everything in their power to get an abortion approved. They traveled vainly to various clinics on the outskirts of North Carolina. They even went to places no human being should ever have to go to, but their fountain of luck ran dry. Hope's fate was sealed. Six months pregnant—trapped—a prisoner of her own body. Hope was carrying a baby forced on her by the beautiful town of Ashbourne Valley, North

Carolina. She was powerless in the face of the law. Whisky granted her some peace of mind—temporary yet cherished nonetheless.

Hope was now seven months pregnant. She barely spoke to Catherine and barely left the hut. Catherine got tired of it all. She could no longer bear the sight of her best friend drowning in booze. She could no longer bear the sight of Hope vomiting her guts out every night just to start over the following day. Hope's carelessness and stubbornness broke Catherine's heart. Although she understood that Hope was in a dark place, she did not approve of her behavior. She found it rather repulsive that Hope would opt to self-destruct, jeopardizing the health of an innocent unborn child in the process.

"Hope! You have got to stop! Enough is enough. This is the hand that was dealt to us, and we will handle it. I am not going to sit here and watch you destroy two lives."

"Cathy! Cathy! Oh, why are you yelling, Cathy? We are good… We are good. We are buddies. I am not drunk. I promise you," slurred Hope, staggering off her feet.

"No, we are not good. We are far from good. You broke my heart, Hope. You truly broke my heart. How can you be so selfish? The poor baby did not ask for any of that," said Catherine. She was distraught, powerless, and more importantly, disappointed.

"Oh! So did I ask for any of it, Cathy? Did I beg them to put a baby inside of me? Fine. Fine. You know what, listen. Just listen. I am just... Wait. No. I am just going to go. You don't have to help me anymore. I am going to go, and you can go too if you want. But we just can't go together. If that makes sense to you," said Hope. That made absolutely no sense to Catherine.

"Go where? Hope, please just stop. Can't you see what you are doing to us? Can't you see what you are doing to yourself? Just hand me the bottle!"

"Don't touch me. I am going home now," said Hope as she walked out of the hut.

Catherine dropped onto her knees. She did not know what to do or say anymore. Where was home? The hut was Hope's home. Where was she off to now? She could not believe Hope would just walk out on her. She got up minutes later and ran outside to get Hope, but it was too late. Hope had vanished into thin air.

"Hope! Hope! Stop it. Come back!" Catherine screamed, running down the streets. "Come back! I promise I won't bother you anymore. Just come back, baby girl. You can drink as much as you want. Just come back." She looked for Hope at every shelter, clinic, and hospital in town. She searched for her at every homeless stronghold, every abandoned house in town. Hope was gone.

Catherine was not herself after Hope disappeared. She tried everything and exhausted all resources. Hope was nowhere to be found. She even went down to the police precinct to report Hope missing. A few weeks went by. She slowly began to lose hope. She knew that every good thing would come to an end, and she was okay with that. Yet a deep sadness entrenched itself within her soul. It was not caused by a selfish desire for companionship. She genuinely worried about the safety of someone she cared for wholeheartedly. She had failed Hope, and that was unforgivable. She blamed herself every day for it.

One Saturday morning, Catherine was awakened by the vibration of her cellphone under her pillow. She jumped up half-asleep and looked. The area code resembled that of her job. She responded frantically.

 "Yes, hello!"

"Good evening, ma'am. We are trying to get in touch with Catherine."

"I am Catherine. Who is this?"

"I am calling from Ashbourne Valley Medical Center. It's in regard to Hope."

"Oh Lord! Is she okay?"

"She's stable right now. She was found unconscious and heavily intoxicated on a sidewalk. We found your number in her purse. Are you able to come to the hospital now, ma'am?"

"Oh my God, Hope, what have you done? Oh Lord! I am on my way!"

Catherine hung up and rushed to the hospital. When she arrived, Hope was asleep. She was hooked to various machines with cables dangling left and right and lights blinking here and there. Catherine dropped to her knees and started crying. Something was terribly wrong; Hope's flat stomach was cause for concern. Catherine feared the worst. Although Hope had been desperate for an abortion, Catherine contemplated time and time again the idea of being a godmother to Hope's child. She was willing and ready to support Hope and help raise this innocent child. The thought of a stillbirth frightened Catherine; her knees weakened.

"This is all my fault. This is all my fault. I failed you, Hope. I should have been more supportive. Look at you! Look what I did to you!" cried Catherine.

"Miss? Are you a family member?" said the attending nurse.

"No! Huh, yes, yes. I am her only family. Is she okay? Where is the baby?"

"She is going to be okay. Her blood pressure was skyrocketing when she got here, but now it's back to normal. Right now, she is under observation. The doctors do not believe there is anything medically wrong with her."

"Okay. But where is the baby?" insisted Catherine, fearing the worst yet hoping for a miracle.

"We were unfortunately unable to save the baby. The fetus was already inert when we got it out. The cause of stillbirth appears to be placental abruption," explained the nurse.

"Placenta what? What is that?"

"It is a condition in which the placenta detaches from the womb before the pregnancy comes to term. We tried everything possible, but it was too late. I am sorry for the loss. Her doctor can give you a more detailed explanation when he gets back. Do you have a contact number for the father?"

"Oh my God. I can't breathe! Hope. My poor Hope. She's going to be devastated. What is she going to do?"

"Ma'am. Any contact number for the father?"

"I already told you I was her only family, didn't I?" said Catherine in an elevated tone of voice, dismissing the nurse's persistent inquiry about the child's father. "I want to be with her. I want to stay with her. Can I stay?" asked Catherine in a more supplicating voice.

"She is resting right now. We had to give her a mild sedative, but if you wish, you can sit with her. I am sure she would appreciate waking up to a friendly, familiar face."

"Thank you!" murmured Catherine. She sat by Hope's bedside and held her hand. She tried to come up with a decent way to break the horrible news to Hope, a way that wouldn't be too crude or too direct. Nothing seemed appropriate. There was no appropriate way to tell a mother about a miscarriage. Although Hope had not wanted to have anything to do with the child, she was a mother nonetheless. Her sanity was already hanging by a very thin thread. The loss of a child was most likely going to be the straw that broke the camel's back. Lost in her thoughts, Catherine dozed off holding Hope's hand.

She was awakened at approximately 1:00 a.m. by a young doctor. He had to be in his early thirties but looked much younger, probably because of his clean-shaven cheeks—or his good genes. A pair of high cheekbones complemented his slightly elongated and chiseled chin. His full eyebrows added a mysterious twist to the deep look in his eyes. Catherine looked up. A rousing sensation roamed up her backbone; the doctor's scintillating emerald eyes were to blame. Catherine caught herself gazing. Her eyes wandered; reality escaped her sight for a split second. She clenched her hands, but the blushing and the quivering gave her away. The doctor picked up on her embarrassment. He got on his knees, grabbed her clenched fist, and tried to comfort her.

"Sorry to wake you up, ma'am. I wanted to introduce myself and see how everyone was doing. I am Dr. Huntelaard. I understand our patient here is family of yours?"

"Hi! Hi! Yes, Doctor. She is. I just don't know how to handle this situation," said Catherine in a bellowing voice. It was hard to tell if she was referring to Hope's situation or her own embarrassing love-at-first-sight situation.

"She is going to be okay, I can assure you of that. Her condition has improved since she arrived. She will be on her feet in no time. I am heading to my office to complete a few charts, but if you need anything, do not hesitate to knock. It's down the hall, fourth door on the left. In the meantime, our nurses are monitoring her closely. She is in good hands."

"Thank you, Doctor. I appreciate your patience."

"No worries at all, ma'am. Tomorrow will be a brighter day."

He walked away and closed the door behind himself. Catherine took a deep, well-needed breath; she had never seen a man so imposing yet so gentle as the young doctor. There was something dangerous about his charisma, something dark and puzzling. As much as she wanted to be there for Hope, it was obvious that the young doctor occupied her most immediate thoughts. The doctor's voice resonated inside her head over and over after he left the room. She had not been involved with a man in a very long time, and she intended to keep it that way. Yet she had already felt her senses weaken in his presence. Her only option was to avoid him at all costs.

Catherine had deep, buried secrets that she had no intention of sharing with any man. Her body craved the touch of a magnificent man to take her breath away. Deep inside, she yearned for that passionate love, but her parents had damaged her self-esteem beyond repair. For the sake of upholding old traditions and archaic beliefs, they had mutilated her sexual organs. She was only twelve years old when it happened, and since that day, she had never ceased to think of herself as incomplete. She never ceased to think of herself as a lesser woman. She battled that feeling of inadequacy throughout her teenage years, only to have her confidence crushed again by her ex-husband, the only man she had ever loved, the only man she had ever been with, a man who would only sleep with her when he was drunk. She remembered those painful nights. She endured his verbal and physical abuse because she believed no other man would want her. She remembered when she had to settle for way less than she deserved because she was too afraid of being alone.

Catherine tried to go back to sleep, to no avail; she had way too much on her mind at this point. She had awakened slumbering memories; the price to pay for such effrontery was heartaches and tears. She was overwhelmed by a wide range of emotions and they were all competing for her flowing tears.

Catherine was too deep in her thoughts to notice Hope opening her eyes. Hope groaned when she saw Catherine crying silently.

"Cathy! Oh, Cathy! I am so sorry! I am okay, my love. Stop the crying now, come on. See. I am all right, babe."

"Hope! You are awake! Oh my God. If you ever scare me like that again, I will kill you myself."

"I am so sorry, Cathy. I know you want what's best for me — what's best for us, the baby and me. I am so sorry for putting you in this predicament. I should have listened. I am sorry. I promise I will listen from now on"

Hope was sincerely sorry. It had taken almost dying to make her realize that Catherine was the only person who cared about her. Seeing Catherine in tears made her realize that she was not alone after all. Catherine wiped off her tears. She struggled to find the words to break the bad news to Hope. She didn't have to. Hope lifted the cover, looked at her stomach, and looked back at Catherine. She then scrutinized the room for a crib or anything of that nature.

"Where's the baby, Cathy? Look at me. Look at me, Catherine. Where is my child? Where is my child? Where is my child?"

The more Hope looked at Catherine, the more upset she got. She looked into Catherine's eyes and unmistakably saw the answer to her question. Her child was gone. She screamed. A deep, painful, cringing shriek escaped her mouth. The sound traveled throughout the hospital's walls like water through a porous rug.

As nurses came running into the room to calm Hope down, Catherine managed to sneak out. She needed some fresh air. She couldn't bear the sight of her friend going from mental breakdown to mental breakdown. She sat on a wooden bench right outside of the hospital and started smoking a cigarette. She had no more tears to shed, but her glassy eyes testified to her deep sadness. Life had taught Catherine that fairness is an elusive and mythical concept. Still, she couldn't bring herself to accept that Hope had to endure so much suffering.

Her cigarette calmed her nerves just enough to give her the strength to go back in. She stopped by the bathroom to wash her face and her mouth. She braced herself for the worst as she pushed open the double door separating the hallway from the patients' rooms. She expected Hope to still be causing a ruckus, but to her great surprise, the floor was quiet. Even the chattering of the ladies at the front desk had stopped. As she approached Hope's room, she felt uneasy about what she saw.

Hope was resting her head on the doctor's lap while he gently massaged her scalp back and forth. She seemed so peaceful. She still had tears in her eyes, but she was no longer kicking and screaming. She was sobbing quietly, holding her stomach. The young doctor had managed to calm her down. Any compassionate doctor would have done exactly what Dr. Huntelaard did. There was nothing inappropriate about it. Yet Catherine's personal feelings hindered her judgment. There was more going on than a good bedside manner—she was sure of it. She caught herself being jealous but fought back the unsettling feeling. She always placed Hope's happiness before her own. That was both her weakness and her strength. She pushed the door and entered the room to let Hope know that she was still around. The creaking sound startled the doctor a little.

"Hey, Hope!" said Catherine, avoiding eye contact with the doctor. "I am here, okay, if you need anything." Hope turned around, acknowledged Catherine's presence with a forced smile, then went back to her original position. Catherine had no idea what the doctor had said to Hope, but it worked. Although still very much hurt, Hope appeared to be accepting her fate. *It is unfortunate that things had to happen in such a tragic fashion,* thought Catherine. *At least she will not have to raise her rapist's child.*

CHAPTER X

***

Hope was admitted to the Ashbourne Medical Center for a few weeks. Her health improved gradually, but her lack of appetite raised some concerns. She lost over thirty pounds in four weeks. She blamed herself for the loss of her child. She became emotionally empty, like a hollow vessel—half afloat, half submerged—at the mercy of the ocean's currents. Her negligence had caused the death of her child. The guilt was eating away at her sanity. She only seemed at peace when Dr. Huntelaard was around. His demeanor alone inspired comfort. He was kind and genuine. Hope was certain that men were conniving by nature, but in the doctor, she saw an exception to that rule. He always knew exactly what to say and exactly when to say it.

"Hello there, strong lady! How are we doing today?" said Dr. Huntelaard.

"I am doing fine, Doctor. I am tired of being in bed all day long, though."

"Yeah, that can be pretty exhausting. You should walk around a bit from time to time."

"Don't think that I haven't tried. Your nurses won't leave me alone. They follow me around like I am some prisoner trying to escape."

"Ah! Yeah, they tend to do that. It's not their fault, though. Hospital policies and all. I will talk to them."

"Thanks, Doctor. I am tired of being constantly watched," said Hope.

She was not being treated like a prisoner. The nurses were concerned that she might attempt to hurt herself. She understood why she was being monitored; she just wanted to see how much the doctor cared. In the evening of that same day, she got out of bed and walked along the hallway. Surprisingly, the nurses kept their distance and let her roam free around the entire maternity ward. She stood on the balcony for a little while, enjoying the view and the fresh air. Catherine had to leave for work, and the doctor was done for the day. She had no one to talk to, so she allowed her mind to wander free. She spent hours trying to give shape to clusters of clouds in the sky but eventually got bored and went back to her room.

The following morning, Dr. Huntelaard had flowers delivered to Hope's room. The card read, "You are stronger than you believe. Speedy recovery, tiger."

She smiled upon reading such a comforting message. *Tiger?* she thought. *What does that mean?* She didn't know what to make of it, but it put a smile on her face. She felt cared for. The first person to hear about the flowers was indeed Catherine. Hope called her minutes after reading the card.

"Hey, Cathy! Guess what happened to me this morning!"

Catherine picked up a happy tone in Hope's voice. It warmed her heart to know that something pleasant had happened to her friend at last.

"Oh, stop torturing me, girl. I don't want to guess. Tell me," replied Catherine.

"Just guess, Cathy, guess. You are no fun."

"Oh God. Fine. You are being discharged today?"

"No! You are way off. Guess again. It's something sweet and silly. And scary."

"Hmm. Sweet, huh? There is a man involved, then."

"Ha ha! You are getting warmer. Keep guessing."

Catherine was glad that her best friend had found some source of excitement, but she was getting a bit anxious. She was impatient by nature, and the guessing game was never fun to her.

"Hope, I am done guessing. Just tell me, girl. Stop teasing."

"Fine. I received some flowers this morning. Can you guess whom they were from?"

"Hope! Jeez, no more guessing, I said," replied Catherine, a little annoyed. She knew exactly whom the flowers were from, and once again, abnormal electrical waves traveled up and down her spine.

"Gosh. Okay, Catherine. I received some flowers from the young doctor. There was a note attached to it in which he called me 'tiger.' It made me very happy. He also told me that I was strong."

"Go, girl! He likes you. You know that, right? He's cute too!" said Catherine.

"You think so? I mean, I don't know. It is his job to be sweet and caring, no?" asked Hope.

"Girl, bedside manners do not extend to flowers and sweet messages. You know it, and I know it."

"I guess you have a point. Is that going to be okay with you, though?"

"With me? Why wouldn't it be okay with me? We are friends, Hope. I want what's best for you."

"You know what I mean, Cathy. Don't play dumb. I have seen how you look at him and how you always seem relieved when he leaves the room."

"Hope, you are reading too much into things. He is cute and successful. Isn't that enough to make any woman feel the way I feel? I will be fine. Better my best friend than some stranger," joked Catherine.

"Thanks, Cathy. It's probably nothing, anyways. He is just being a gentleman. Thanks for having my back. I don't know what I would do without you."

"You are welcome, baby girl. We are all we have got," said Catherine. They got off the phone, and Catherine proceeded to do some chores around the hut. She needed to keep her mind occupied.

The flowers became a routine. Hope's health had improved drastically. She was still being monitored due to her fragile mental state and her lack of appetite, but she didn't get to see the doctor as much as she wanted to. Yet flowers were delivered to her room every morning at the exact same time. The notes got sweeter and sweeter every day. She wanted to see him and have a conversation about the flowers, but it was almost as if he was avoiding her. Another doctor, much older, would check on her from time to time. One night, she finally gathered the courage to inquire about the young doctor.

"Excuse me. Can I ask you a question? What happened to my previous doctor? Is he on vacation or something?" Hope asked the doctor as he checked her vitals.

"Hmm. I am not sure who you are referring to. We rotate quite a bit on this floor. You have a name?" responded the doctor, seemingly bothered by the question.

Hope felt stupid. She didn't remember the name of her admirer. He had mentioned his name when they first met, but it escaped her. All the notes were signed "Doc." She was so embarrassed that she completely forgot that she was in the middle of a conversation.

"Is it something that I am doing wrong or that you don't like?" asked the doctor.

"Oh, no. I am so sorry you feel that way. Everything is fine. I was just being curious. I didn't know you guys rotated."

The new doctor acquiesced and walked out of the room after signing her chart. Hope's innocuous question had wounded his ego a bit. She also made a fool of herself by developing a strong interest in a man whose name she could not even remember. She was aware of the danger of getting attached too quickly. She just couldn't help it. His dark, mysterious personality scared her but intrigued her even more. Her doubts and uncertainties were driving her crazy. She wanted to either confirm a mutual attraction or move on. She thought about asking the other nurses about the doctor, but she did not. It would have been unwise to let them know of her interest in Dr. Huntelaard. They all seemed to be drooling over him when he walked by.

Thursday morning at 7:00 a.m. sharp, a young delivery guy walked in with some pink orchids and a miniature teddy bear. From her window, Hope watched him sign in at the front desk and walk his way to her room. The flowers caught the attention of every woman on the floor. Jealousy filled the room, and Hope enjoyed it very much. She enjoyed being the center of attention once again. It made her feel womanly again, and it made her feel confident again—to a certain extent. She wasn't vain or cocky. She was grateful that a man was interested in her.

"Good morning, lucky lady," said the delivery guy in a deep accented voice.

"Good morning," responded Hope cheerfully.

"Here go your flowers, and today you have a teddy bear to go with them," said the boy as he placed the flower vase on Hope's nightstand.

"Thank you. These flowers always make my day. I wanted to ask you—is there a return address?"

"A return address? You don't want them, ma'am? Oh, I will take them from you if you wish. My girlfriend would love them," joked the delivery guy again.

"Oh no. I do love them and definitely want them. I was curious about what would happen to them if you show up one day and I am gone."

"Oh, I guess that's a good question. Well, we don't have a return address per se, but we have a phone number. We would call the sender and ask him if he wants them delivered somewhere else."

"Ah, okay. Makes sense. Thank you."

"Not a problem, ma'am. Can you sign right here for me, please?"

"Sure," she said. She signed the confirmation receipt and handed it back to the guy.

"Thanks, ma'am. You have a wonderful day now, and I hope you enjoy the flowers. They are wonderful."

She was disappointed because she hadn't gotten the answer she was expecting. She was so certain that there would be a return address on file or some way to contact the doctor. Wait! But there was a way to contact the sender, a more convenient way.

"Excuse me. Can I bother you one more time before you go?" said Hope to the young guy.

"Sure. What is it?"

"I was about to call him and say thank you, but I realized that I had reset my phone yesterday and lost all my contacts. Would you be a sweetheart and give me his phone number again?"

"We are not allowed to share clients' information, especially for anonymous deliveries. I can make an exception for you, though. If anything happens, you didn't get it from me."

"I really appreciate it. You are a lifesaver."

"Don't mention it," he said as he handed her the doctor's contact information.

Hope rushed to the telephone to call the doctor then froze. What would she do if another woman picked up? What if the doctor was not interested? What if he was just being nice, like all doctors should? She could come up with what-ifs all day long. At the end of the day, she would still be clueless. Hope opted for certainty over speculations; she dialed the number.

"Huntelaard residence, Harry speaking."

"Hello. Hi. Hi, Doctor. It's Hope. Hope from the hospital."

"Hope! What a pleasant surprise. Is everything okay? I heard you were getting discharged soon."

"Everything is fine. I am sorry for the early phone call. I just wanted to say thank you for the orchids. And the roses before them."

"Oh! You liked them? Good. I am glad. Wait! How did you get my number?"

"Yes, I loved them all. I am starting to run out of places to put them, though," teased Hope nervously. She was trying to avoid discussing the scheme she'd employed to get the phone number.

"Very funny. You still haven't told me how you got my home number. Nobody at work has it."

"Ah! I will make you a deal. If you tell me why you abandoned me, I will tell you how I got your number."

"I did not abandon you, silly. Aren't the flowers proof enough that I care about your recovery? I got transferred to our uptown branch. That's why I have not been around much."

"You did not stop by to say hello… or goodbye," complained Hope.

"I wanted to, but it happened so suddenly, and I didn't want to make you feel uncomfortable."

"Whatever you say. Excuses, that's all I am hearing."

"Don't be like that, Hope. You know what? I will make it up to you. We are going out for dinner as soon as you get discharged. How does that sound?"

"Sounds great. I hope you don't have any plans tomorrow night, then, because I am getting discharged tomorrow morning," said Hope apprehensively.

She wanted to meet him as soon as possible. She was a little pushy because she wanted to make sure he was really into her. A moment of silence fell; Hope feared that she might have scared him away by being so forceful. She waited an eternity for a response, biting her bottom lip in anger and blaming herself for ruining it all.

"Sorry for the little wait. I had to check my planner and send out a couple of emails. It seems like all my plans got magically canceled. So we are on for tomorrow night, seven o'clock at the Concord. Should I pick you up, or would you rather meet me there?"

"The Concord? Can't we meet somewhere else? It's a little out of my way."

"We could meet somewhere else, but we won't. The waterfront view over there is so peaceful. It reminds me of the look in your eyes the first time I touched your hair. You will love it."

Hope wanted to avoid the Concord at all costs because she knew how awkward it would be to run into Catherine. Also, she worried that the owner's son would recognize her and ruin the date. Yet she didn't want to push it, so she gave in.

"The Concord it is, then. I will be there at seven o'clock, sir. I hope you don't intend on making me blush tomorrow night like you just did," said Hope.

"Great! I am so tempted to assure you that I won't make you blush, but I refuse to make a promise that I can't keep. See you tomorrow night, tiger."

"Tomorrow night then, Dr. Huntelaard," replied Hope, teasingly.

CHAPTER XI

Hope hung up the phone. She sat on her bed and played with her pillow pensively. She was excited about her date. She had no memory of any prior date or a consensual relationship. She had no memory of any other man giving her goose bumps and butterflies. In the midst of all that excitement, she hadn't thought about what she was going to wear. The doctor was used to seeing her in patient gowns. She wanted to make a shockingly great first impression. She had packed up her old dresses and never hoped to use any of them ever again. She couldn't use any of them even if she wanted to. None of them would fit her. She was a little insecure about her body. She took comfort in the fact that the doctor had seen her at her worst and still wanted to talk to her. Daisy-print socks and pink-dotted patient gowns are not particularly sexy.

She wanted to call Catherine right away and tell her about the date, but she resolved to have that conversation in person. The following day, Hope woke up earlier than usual. She had finished gathering her belongings when the nurse came barging into her room.

"Well, how are you feeling today, flower girl?"

"Not too bad."

"Well, I have news that's going to make you feel much better. The doctor just cleared you for discharge."

"Wonderful! Thank you!"

"No problem. If you want to take your flowers with you, we have a van that can take them to your home free of charge. Make sure you stop by the front desk when you are ready to go. We will give you your discharge papers and a follow-up interview."

"Oh no, there's no need for a van. I will take what I can. Most of them have started to die anyway."

"All right, then. I will be outside. Take your time."

She wanted to take all her flowers with her. She was going to miss her daily deliveries. Yet she had nowhere to put them. The little hut was already packed, and she didn't want to throw her happiness in Catherine's face. Hope hated herself for leaving some of her flowers behind. She insisted that they be

131

thrown out immediately. She was worried that the doctor would stop by and see them. After packing up everything that two hands could carry, she called Catherine to give her the good news.

"Hey, Cathy. I am getting out today! Are you busy? Can you come get me?"

"Oh great! I am coming from a job interview. I am not too far from you, Hope. I will be there in fifteen minutes, okay?"

Catherine was in front of the hospital fifteen minutes after hanging up the phone. She was so excited to finally have her friend back. The glow on her face touched Hope deeply and made her feel guilty. Catherine hailed a cab over on Elm Street. They filled the trunk with flower vases and placed their bags against them to keep them from tipping over. Hope was particularly fond of her last delivery; she took the vase of orchids with her inside of the cab.

"So are you excited, Hope? I am free today. We should have a picnic at the park to celebrate."

"I am very excited! I missed you so much! The smell of the hospital was driving me crazy, Cathy. And the nurses are so mean; they hated me."

"No! Don't think like that, girl. They do not hate you. They are just old and grouchy."

"Even the young ones are mean. But anyways, that's over now. There's something I want to run by you, Cathy. We can talk about it at the park."

"Girl! Why are you always teasing my curiosity? We are not going to wait. What is it?"

"Well, I talked to the doctor yesterday, and…"

"And?"

"Gosh Cathy, will you let me finish? we are going out tonight. He wants to take me to the Concord. I don't think it's a good idea because you work there, and I don't want to make it awkward for you."

"You have got to stop this nonsense, Hope. I am irrelevant. I can bet you he doesn't remember meeting me. You are making it awkward now by bringing it up constantly," said Catherine.

"Sorry, I didn't mean to upset you, Cathy. I was worried about the effect this will have on our friendship. That's all."

"Well, you have got to stop patronizing me, Hope. I am still here for you, aren't I? How many times do I have to tell you that I don't care for him like you seem to believe I do?"

"Okay. Okay, Cathy. I am sorry. That's done with, then. Sorry, I won't bring it up again."

"It's okay. Oh wait! So, we have got to get you a dress then, Hope. What are you going to wear?" said Catherine.

"I don't know. My dresses won't fit me; we sold most of them anyways."

"Driver, change of plans. Can you drop us on the corner of Front and Brentwood?" said Catherine to the taxi driver.

"Brentwood," exclaimed Hope. "Why are we going to this part of town?"

"There's a thrift shop right on the corner. We are going to get you a nice dress, girl. Sit back, and let me worry about everything."

Catherine was very sweet and helpful by nature. Yet in this instance, she was being overzealous. Her sudden outpouring of generosity and care was her way of coping with that intense upsurge of envy traveling through her mind. Her ability to drastically change her emotional response was commendable.

134

She never gave Hope a reason to doubt her sincerity even though she was not entirely sincere. She was very much bothered by this situation. She shifted her attention to Hope, thus neglecting or rather repressing her personal feelings. Deep inside, she wished it was her receiving the flowers. She wished it was her going on a date with the charming young doctor. Hope and Catherine were both battling embedded insecurities. The prospect of a date was a boost to Hope's confidence, yet the feeling of rejection intensified Catherine's self-doubt. She helped Hope because she cared. She also helped because being helpful was her way of casting a cape over the darkness in her soul.

They finally arrived at the thrift shop, and Catherine paid the taxi a little extra to wait for them. He didn't seem in a hurry as he parked his rugged SUV near the fire hydrant and turned on his hazard lights. It took a little convincing to get Hope to entrust her flowers in the hands of the cabbie. They walked inside the thrift shop.

"Let's try to find you a decent dress for a decent price," joked Catherine. That was another way of saying "a great dress for very cheap." It took them only thirty minutes to pick out a dress. Hope was not picky, and she needed to get back to the comfort of her bed as soon as possible. They agreed on a light-beige dress, paid for it, and rushed back to the taxi.

"That was quick, by women's standards," joked the cabbie as they got back in the taxi. He didn't get any reaction at first, so he assumed that his joke had fallen on deaf ears, but it had not. Hope and Catherine had both been victims of gender stereotyping. They had both been deeply wounded by men and their egos. They had both suffered from prejudicial treatments based on their gender. They did not find sexist stereotypical jokes amusing. In fact, Catherine found his joke particularly distasteful. She loathed men who perpetuated the circle of sexism through innuendos and jokes. The cab driver exemplified exactly the type of men Catherine despised.

"What did you just say? Oh no, you did not say what I just heard! Open your trunk, please! We are getting out. Let's go, Hope."

"Hey, come on, ladies. It was a little lighthearted joke."

"Open your trunk please, sir. We need to get our flowers," said Hope in a firm tone of voice. She had realized that Catherine was extremely offended by the driver's remark. She jumped in to avoid a back-and-forth argument. She also found the remark distasteful, but she was too tired to even bother to say something back to the cabbie. Deep inside, she was glad that Catherine had reacted to it. They removed their things from the trunk, and the cabbie drove away angrily. Catherine was fuming. The sexist joke had clearly struck a raw nerve. She'd had enough of the toleration of bigotry and the marginalization of women. She'd had enough of innuendos. She'd had enough of sexism disguised behind silly jokes, enough of normalized prejudices.

Hope managed to calm her down and get her in another cab. Their day had essentially been ruined. Catherine no longer wanted to go picnicking. Hope also wanted to go home and take a nap. She wanted to get her beauty rest before the date, so she wasn't too disappointed by the idea of staying home. They got out of the taxi a block away from their hut, as usual. Catherine made several trips, carrying flowers and food while Hope stood watch. They finally got everything into their little hut, and Hope went straight to bed. Their bed wasn't as fancy as the hospital bed, but it felt more comfortable. There was no place like home. She no longer had to worry about judgmental eyes peeping through her window. There was nobody around to gossip about her situation.

Hope slept like a baby. She woke up at around four o'clock in the afternoon to find Catherine cooking scrambled eggs and bacon bites. It must have been the delightful aroma of bacon that woke her up. She was in the middle of the sweetest dream, but her nostrils knew how to appreciate the smell of juicy bacon bites. She sat on the bed for a few minutes, savoring the whiff coming into the hut from a crack in the window. She heard the sizzling, and it was almost as if she could already taste the slight saltiness of bacon on her tongue. She smiled at how grateful she was to have met Catherine.

"Catherine, why are you cooking breakfast at four o'clock in the afternoon?" yelled Hope from inside the hut.

"You can grab a plate, or you can stay in there and nag me with that silly smirk on your face," said Catherine.

"You can't even see me. How do you know I have a silly smirk on my face?"

"Because you always have a silly smirk on your face when I make bacon!"

"So bacon again, huh? You never get tired of eating pork, do you?" teased Hope again as she stepped out of the hut. She enjoyed pulling Catherine's leg, and Catherine did not mind it at all.

"I will stop eating it when you do. Here!" replied Catherine as she handed a plate to Hope. "Eat so you aren't all gassy tonight and won't embarrass yourself in front of your date. I doubt he will be as tolerant as

I am when you start breaking wind in the middle of the dinner, Stinky."

Catherine was trying to cheer her up. Hope didn't laugh at her joke. Her palms started sweating, and Catherine noticed the plate shaking a bit. She had forgotten that she had a date, and now that she was reminded of it, she had butterflies in her stomach.

"Hope, cut the shit, girl. You will be fine. It is just dinner, and you have nothing to lose," said Catherine in a motherly tone of voice.

"I know. I know. He's scary, you know—in a good way but still scary. The way he looks at me makes me feel like he can read my mind," replied Hope. Worrisome thoughts took a toll on Hope's mind, so she decided to just stop overthink and go with the flow. Catherine was right, after all. She had nothing to lose.

Hope had just lost her child. She should have been sad, crying, grieving. Yet she was out there, ready to enjoy life. She owed that to the irresistible charisma of Dr. Huntelaard. The excitement that was building up inside of her was uncontainable. Her desire to be in the company of the charming doctor superseded her sadness and her fears. She had promised herself to never get close to any man. Ha! Empty promises. She spent the rest of the afternoon joking around with Catherine until it was time to get ready for her date.

CHAPTER XII

Hope arrived at the restaurant half an hour early. She did not want to keep Harry waiting, nor did she want him to see her getting off the downtown blue-line bus. It didn't take a genius to know that the blue line ran only through the least frequented parts of town. She went into the bathroom to fix up her light makeup. As she walked out of the bathroom and into the dining area, she found herself face-to-face with Harry. He was wearing a dark-gray button-up fitted shirt with dark-blue slacks. He looked tall and mysterious, as usual, but this time Hope saw something else in his eyes. She saw vulnerability. She saw wonder in his eyes.

"You look like a nightingale, a nightingale above the clouds," he whispered in her ear as he hugged her.

Hope could feel his heartbeat on her breast. His hand shivered a bit as he touched her right shoulder. She had never seen him nervous and unsure before. She was used to him being dominant. She enjoyed seeing a softer side of him. Harry blushed as Hope fixed his collar after the hug. He was so good at disguising his emotions that one would think he was naturally red cheeked. He reached for Hope's hand, and they walked together to their reserved table on the waterfront.

Hope's confidence skyrocketed as she walked past a handful of young ladies in their early twenties, sipping fancy wine. She felt their eyes affixed to her. She reached out and held onto Harry's arm as if she wanted to let everyone know that he was unavailable. Her cheap beige dress embraced her contours and exposed her legs from her knees down. She was dominant in her high heels. At this very moment, she understood that the price of her dress was irrelevant. The only thing that mattered was that she was comfortable in her skin and comfortable with what she was wearing. She was interrupted in her thoughts by the doctor's regretful voice, almost whispering as he pulled out her chair.

"Sorry for being a little late. How long have been waiting on me?" he asked.

"Oh, not too long. Just long enough to reconsider my decision to come here, though," said Hope fretfully.

"Well, you are still here. That must mean something."

"I was actually on my way home from the bathroom when you ran into me. In a sense, your timing is impeccable." Joked Hope.

"Ha! very funny. Well, I am glad I caught you right on time."

"I am equally glad. Although I still don't know why we had to meet here."

"I can tell you why. Look at that exquisite view. Look at the sun looming behind the horizon. If this isn't the most beautiful sight, after your eyes, then I don't know what is."

Hope giggled. The doctor was getting comfortable. His natural charm slowly crept back. Hope did not know how to respond to such an elaborate compliment.

"Have you been here before?" inquired Hope.

"I actually have. It is one of my favorite places to dine."

"Favorite place to take unaware women and lure them into falling for your fallacious charm?" asked Hope with a smile. She wanted the doctor to think she was joking. But was she really joking? That remains a mystery.

"I figured that is what you were getting at. You are the first person I have brought here. I usually dine alone."

"And you expect me to believe that a successful, charming, and handsome doctor dines alone in a place filled with bachelorettes?" asked Hope.

"I am sensing a bit of animosity and sarcasm here. Have I given you the impression that I shouldn't be trusted or believed?" responded Dr. Huntelaard defensively.

"No animosity at all. I was simply inquiring out of curiosity. I would have never pictured you as a loner; you seem so friendly and full of life."

"I do dine alone more often than not. And when I am not alone, I am with business partners. I can see why that's hard for you to believe, but it is the truth," explained Dr. Huntelaard. His tone seemed sincere.

Hope's skepticism was fathomable. The only memories Hope had of men were awful. She had only been around cheaters, drunks, and misogynistic bigots. She had only been a fantasy, the object of sexual desires. She was paid to entertain men, and men were paid to rip her dignity out of her guts.

Harry understood Hope's worries. He realized that it would take patience and understanding to get Hope to let down her guard. Getting her to come out on a date was already a small victory and a major step toward building trust. Thankfully, patience seemed to be Harry's forte. He had no intention of rushing her, and he was more than willing to walk her through the process of dating.

When it comes to matters of the heart, there are no quadrants or formulas that can be used to measure the truthfulness of words and actions. It is always a gamble, an educated guess at best. For Hope, it was pure gamble; she lacked the dating experience required to make an educated guess.

"Hello there. How are we doing on this lovely evening? I am Kate, and I will be your server for the night. What can I get you guys started with?"

"I will have a glass of water and a dirty martini for now," replied Harry.

"A glass of white wine for me, please. And we will try your lemon shrimp appetizers," said Hope confidently. Catherine had told her exactly what to order.

"Very good choice; they are also my favorites. I will be right back with your drinks," said the waitress.

Hope looked at her walking away in her tight black pants and her little teenager blazer. She was elegantly dressed. Hope felt a bit threatened. She looked at Harry. He appeared completely uninterested in the waitress's round bottom and ample chest.

"Lemon shrimp, huh? Good choice. So how are you enjoying your night so far?" said Harry as he reached over for Hope's hands.

"Pretty good so far, but the night is young," said Hope.

"Touché. The night is young, indeed. So why don't you tell me a bit about yourself? Generic question, I know. Generic but necessary."

"You should lead the way like the true gentleman you seem to be."

"Well, there isn't much to say. Born in New Jersey. Parents moved to North Carolina when I was seven. The rest is typical. College, medical school, parties here and there, and here I am, Dr. Harry Huntelaard."

"Come on. You know darn well you are leaving the juicy details out."

"No juicy details. I have been single for a little while now, so I guess I have done what most single men do. Your turn now."

"I have to be honest with you. I do not know much about myself. I suffer from retrograde amnesia. I only have recollection of the past few years or so."

"Oh no. Sorry to hear that. What happened? Car accident?"

"I wish I knew. I woke up one day in the middle of nowhere, and everything was blank."

"That is unfortunate. Well, we will make great memories to replace the ones you have lost."

"Oh, will we now? So confident!"

"We sure will."

"Don't make promises you can't keep."

"It's not a promise; it's a wish. But I am sure you will make my wish come true."

The doctor's wit was overwhelming, but Hope liked his ease with words. She liked the fact that he would always find a way to turn any conversation into a subtle compliment. She felt a sense of relief after talking to Harry. She wanted him to know of her condition, but she was afraid that retrograde amnesia would be a deal breaker. Luckily, her fears were unfounded. They spent the rest of the night throwing playful jabs at each other.

The waitress finally brought over their food. Harry unbuttoned the top button of his shirt and began to savor his juicy steak. Hope felt slightly aroused. The sight of his broad chest was exquisitely torturous. She had been in the presence of many attractive men before while at the tavern. None of them ever caused her to twitch so much. There was something much deeper than physical attraction with Harry. It was a natural, organic connection. She had never felt so alive inside, so warm yet so cold. It was such an electrifying feeling to desire someone so much that the body became unable to contain the influx of titillating sensations. Her pulse raged at the core of her femininity. The constant throbbing at the junction of her thighs was like a distress message. Her feet touched Harry's feet under the table, sending shivers up her spine. She apologized.

"I am so sorry. I had to stretch my legs. They start to go to sleep when I sit for too long."

"No, no. Don't apologize. I always wondered how women manage with these high heels. Don't get me wrong—they look sexy, but they also look uncomfortable."

"Yeah, they can be quite uncomfortable. The sacrifices we make to feel pretty, right?" teased Hope, still in a flirtatious mood.

"Well, your sacrifices are appreciated although not needed. You are breathtakingly gorgeous with or without heels," said Harry as he set down his drink and smiled.

"You promised not to make me blush, and here you go again," said Hope.

"I made no such promise. I will promise you a foot massage, though, on our second date since you just confessed that these shoes are taking a toll on your pretty feet."

"Hmm. A second date! You waste no time! Well, I think I would enjoy a foot massage very much," said Hope nervously. She was a bit concerned because she knew things could escalate really quickly from a foot massage. She did not want to be a mood killer, so she went with the flow. It was almost eleven at night, and the restaurant was starting to look deserted. Neither of them wanted to leave. Neither of them wanted to end a night so simple yet so magical.

"Excuse me, guys. The kitchen is closing in fifteen minutes. Would you guys like to order anything else?" said the young waitress, disrupting a gazing contest between Harry and Hope.

"Oh, no thanks, dear. We are getting ready to leave soon," said Harry.

The excitement of date night had passed, and the idea of going home had Hope pensive. She was wondering whether she should tell Harry about her living situation. He seemed like an understanding guy, and he was really interested in Hope. Was he interested enough to overlook the fact that Hope lived under a bridge? Was he interested enough to overlook the fact that Hope showered in public restrooms? Hope was not ready to find out. She opted to keep her secret to herself a little longer. She had no intention of ruining her little moment of joy with idle chatter and tales of her misfortune. She gracefully turned down Harry's offer to take her home. She was exhausted. A ride home would have been ideal, but she was not quite ready to open up about her homelessness.

It was one o'clock in the morning when she got home. She tried her best not to wake up Catherine. To her great surprise, Catherine was wide awake. She was reading an old version of Simone de Beauvoir's *The Second Sex* for the hundredth time. This damp, stained book with a creased cover was to Catherine what the Holy Bible is to the Pope.

Catherine was always boggled by the way men tend to disparage women. This book offered an in-depth analysis of the complexity of gender roles—a semblance of explanation that Catherine longed for. The first few chapters had been a transforming experience for her. She'd needed a voice to speak for her, a voice to speak to her, a voice to speak of her. Simone de Beauvoir was that voice.

Catherine put down her book as soon as Hope entered the room. Nothing beat juicy post-first-date gossip.

CHAPTER XIII

***

Hope walked past Catherine with a smirk on her face, slowly removed her heels, and slid off her dress. She grabbed a wet towel and wiped the light makeup off her face. Not once did she make eye contact with Catherine.

"Hope! I know you see me sitting right here. Don't make me ask," said Catherine.

"Oh Lord, girl. Why are you still up, anyway? Go to sleep. There's nothing to tell. It was just dinner and small talk," said Hope, laughing.

"Is that why you are blushing just by talking about it?" observed Catherine.

"Fine. I know you are not going to let me sleep until I spill my guts anyways. It was okay, Cathy. I was really nervous at first, but then it all became natural. He was kind and sweet. We talked a lot, but I don't recall anything we talked about except that I may be getting a foot massage on our second date. He seems really interested."

"A second date! That's awesome. I doubt he will only massage your feet," joked Catherine as she pinched Hope on her arms. "I am glad you enjoyed yourself. Be careful, hon. Move slow, you know."

"Yeah, I will. I am just glad to be home. He gets me so weak in my knees," said Hope. They fell asleep chatting about the dos and don'ts of that prospective second date.

It had now been eight months since Hope and Harry started to date exclusively. He showered her with attention and flowers. His warmth was her sweet obsession. His smile was her sunshine; his kisses became her addiction. Hope spent most of her evenings at Harry's apartment, but she always rushed home at night. She could never bring herself to leave Catherine alone; She felt obliged to keep her company throughout the night.

Harry understood and respected such a strong bond of friendship. He never complained, not once. His patience was eventually rewarded. On February fourteenth, Catherine signed up for a double shift; she always worked double shifts on Valentine's Day to keep her mind busy and avoid dwelling on her loneliness. Hope was free to do as she pleased with her night. They got back to Harry's place fairly late after their Valentine's Day shenanigans.

"Hey, beautiful! It's getting late. Are you sure you don't want me to drop you off tonight? It's probably not safe to take the bus this late at night," inquired Harry that night.

"I am staying here tonight," said Hope confidently. She caught Harry off guard. He could not hide the ray of excitement that spread across his face.

"Oh! You are?" inquired Harry.

"If that's okay with you, of course," replied Hope.

"Of course. Why wouldn't it be okay with me?" said Harry excitedly as he sat down on the couch next to Hope and wrapped his arms around her.

Harry kissed Hope sweetly. He bit her left earlobe and slid his left arm under her shirt. Hope trembled. She was losing control; her feet left the ground momentarily. Harry continued to passionately explore her cleavage with his tongue.

"Stop, stop, stop," whispered Hope desperately in Harry's ears as he began to unbutton her pants. Harry kissed her lips passionately as if he was trying to shut her up. He continued to unzip her pants. A sentiment of deep fear and anxiety invaded Hope's mind.

"Stop, Harry!" said Hope firmly as she jumped off the couch. She was sweating profusely, and her shaky hands struggled to zip her pants back up.

"What's wrong? Are you okay? What did I do now?" asked Harry, confused.

"I am so sorry, Harry. It's not you, it's me. It's me. Please forgive me. I am sorry," sobbed Hope. She dropped to her knees and grabbed Harry's hands. Harry slowly got up, picked her up off the floor, and carried her into the bedroom. He placed the cover over her, kissed her forehead, and lay next to her.

"It's okay, baby. It's going to be okay," he said. "We can wait."

Months went by. Harry exemplified the very notion of patience. He moved at Hope's pace and lived by Hope's wishes. Hope had a growing desire to let Harry explore the wonders of her temple but she often found herself struggling to overcome the crippling fear that paralyzed her every time she thought about it.

Eventually, she decided that it was time to conquer the demons of her past. She waited and waited for Harry to initiate things, but he never showed a whim of desire to discover her innermost treasure.

Hope grew weary of waiting on Harry to make a move. She grew hungry for his warmth inside of her. She started to feel a bit self-conscious. Harry's neglect made her feel undesirable. She decided to take matters into her own hands.

At the dawn of Spring, on a beautiful Thursday afternoon, the couple met at the Ashbourne National Park for a picnic. Everyone seemed to be making their way home when Harry and Hope arrived by the small lake, on the south side of the park. They enjoyed being near the water. The lake had deep significance for the both of them. For Hope, it provided a sense of security and comfort. For Harry, it signified serenity and romance.

A playful pair of swans sailed back and forth, feet away from them. Harry brought the biscuits and the buns, and Hope brought the wine and the blanket. They frolicked on the soft grass for hours. They lost themselves in the natural beauty surrounding them. The strikingly colorful foliage of a nearby weeping willow tree was a sight for sore eyes. There was a pair of hawks perched on a London planetree. Nesting birds sang their tunes in tandem. Hope felt at home; nature was her element. They enjoyed endless banter for hours.

The sun eventually sank behind some nimbus clouds that came out of nowhere. It was getting dark, and the park was deserted. This ecliptic environment was all the encouragement Hope needed. She climbed on top of Harry and began to kiss his lips. Her mouth ventured to Harry's neck, on which she laid some wet kisses. She then ran her tongue up his neck, slowly breathing into his ears. He shivered slightly. She unbuttoned his shirt slowly. The sight of his broad hairy chest sent radiating heat waves throughout her entire body. She continued to kiss him until his stiffness began to press against her body. She found this feeling very comforting and pleasurable. She smiled as his manhood poked her lower stomach, but he was too far gone to notice that smile. His eyes were tightly closed. His mouth, halfway open, was waiting—begging—for Hope to taste him again and again. His bottom lip trembled every time her hips engaged in a thrusting up-and-down motion. His cold hands clasped her lower back like those of a dying man grabbing onto the elixir of life. As he seemed to be losing control, Hope licked the palm of her left hand, slid it into his already unbuttoned pants, and reached for his soul. Harry jumped, grabbing her hand firmly.

"We should not do that," he said, out of breath and sweating.

Hope had reached her breaking point. The buildup was perfect, the mood was set, and everything was enchanting. She simply could not understand why he had to stop her.

"Why would you turn me down and make me feel like shit? Am I not good enough for you? Do I not turn you on?" she screamed, furious and confused.

The reaction she anticipated from Harry was not the reaction she got. Harry turned pale, as if life had left his body. He completely froze, and a tremor of confusion traveled through his body. He looked at Hope with worry in his eyes. It had started to drizzle by then, making this standoff more dramatic. It was almost as if the gods were adding the missing touch to an almost perfect scene of confusion and drama.

"Hope! Why are you screaming? I apologize if I made you feel like I am not into you. I can assure you that I have never been into anyone the way I am into you. I only wanted to wait until you were comfortable. You were upset the first time I tried, so I figured I would wait until we get married or something. I did not want you to feel like you had to do it just to please me." His voice was trembling, filled with emotion. His face was crimson red.

By then, the heavens had opened up. The light drizzling had turned into a downpour. The sky was being ripped apart by thunder, and each string of lightning emphasized the redness of Harry's face.

160

Hope discerned a river of tears rolling down Harry's cheeks, mixed with rain and sweat. She was overwhelmed by guilt, overwhelmed by the forced confession of possible marriage. She was overwhelmed because she didn't know how to handle a crying man, a man consumed by emotions. She was so used to men claiming to be—or trying to be—emotionally sterile. She froze in the face of the most powerful display of emotion exhibited by a man toward her. She tried to talk. Her crackly voice barely reached Harry's ears.

Hope was completely drenched. Her raging hormones and the cold rain conspired to harden her nipples. They were almost ripping through her shirt. She approached Harry nervously, fearing that she had ruined everything. She reached for his trembling arm, but he gently slapped her hand away. Before she realized what was happening, Harry gently grabbed her by her throat. He kissed her with so much passion that their lips became one. Like a raging bull lunging at a red cape, he picked her up with one hand while ripping off her blouse with the other. Her senses spiked at the speed of light. It was no longer that slow buildup she'd experienced earlier. It was full-blown, passionate, mad, uncontrollably wild lovemaking. He took her hard nipples in his mouth, leaving her gasping for air and licking her dried-up lips. How could her lips be dry in such a downpour of rain? Only the gods of sex had an answer to such a mind-boggling question, yet dried they were. Her wetness dripped down her thighs. His left hand began to explore beneath her miniskirt. His fingers mimicked the periodic motion of a rocking chair.

"I can't feel my face," she murmured, but he placed a finger in her mouth, forcing her to almost choke on her words. In a matter of seconds, he had taken control over her body. She allowed him to domineer her senses. He put her down then flipped her around, and she leaned against a young baobab tree with her back arched at a perfect angle. Harry began to kiss her lower back, slowly biting her sides from time to time. He tongued the back of her neck, making his way to her earlobes and then her lips. She was so lost under his touch that she didn't notice him taking off his pants. She gasped for air as he entered her world for the very first time. They were now one. They connected in the most electrifying way. Each stroke sent electrical waves through her spine and down her knees. Her toes curled up. Harry grabbed the arch of her back and made sure she felt all of him. Nothing could take away this magic that was brewing inside of her. Nothing could stop Harry from striking her inner ego with his engorged phallus over and over—not the outpouring of rain, not the enraged thunderstorm, not even the string of lightnings ripping through the sky.

Typical, predictable—steamy lovemaking under the rain, in a public place—reckless and wild. Is the writer so uninspired that he had to disguise his lack of wit behind common fantasies? Or maybe fantasies exist so they can be lived, and Hope lived hers wholly. As time went by, Harry grew fonder and fonder of Hope. He was falling, and he was falling hard; so was Hope. She was trying to hold back. She did not know how Harry would react to her living situation. She felt obliged to come clean and tell him everything. It was getting serious, and she did not want her secret to destroy what she had going on. Besides, she wanted to be herself. She wanted to feel happy and free.

She showed up unannounced at Harry's apartment on a gloomy Friday evening. He let her in then went back to the kitchen to finish cooking his alfredo chicken. Hope had never seen a happier man in her life, singing and cooking, sipping wine and eye-flirting. She was about to break his heart. The thought of him being heartbroken saddened her deeply. Yet she knew she had no choice; she had to come clean.
Harry finally emerged out of the kitchen in a pair of dark shorts. A greenish apron covered his chest, leaving his shoulders exposed. He was holding Hope's plate in one hand and a bottle of red wine in the other. As he handed her the plate, she grabbed his hand.

"Harry, sit with me for a minute. I have something to tell you," she said.

"Woman, nothing can be more pressing than my food right now. Give me five minutes."

"Harry, stop being foolish, please. I need to talk to you now."

"How am I being foolish? I have got to get my food. You don't want me to eat?" asked Harry jokingly.

"Harry, Jesus! Not everything is a joke. I am trying to have a serious, difficult conversation. Can you please just sit next to me and listen?" said Hope.

"All right, then. Geez. What is it that could not wait two more minutes?" he said as he sat down. He was a little annoyed by Hope's undertone.

"All right. I want to tell you something that I should have told you when we first went out. I was scared that you would judge me, so I chickened out."

"What is it you want to tell me, Hope?" he said, a little annoyed.

"Well, I know you never insisted on coming over to my place, and I appreciate you for that. I want to be honest with you. I never invited you over because I

164

don't have a home. I share a homeless shack with Catherine under the bridge on Queen Street."

"I know."

"You know? What do you mean you know? What exactly do you know?"

"I know where you live, Hope. I am sorry, but I did not want to be the one to bring it up."

"How do you know? Catherine was running her mouth again, wasn't she?"

"No. I never talked to your friend. That first night at the Concord, I was worried because it was really late. I followed you to make sure you got to the bus station safe. Once I saw you getting on the downtown bus, I got even more worried, so I followed the bus. I know it's creepy, but I needed to know that you had gotten home safe."

"Why didn't you ever tell me anything?"

"Because you never told me anything, Hope. I mean, can you blame me for not telling you that I knew about your secret that you were too ashamed to tell me about?"

Hope was speechless. She wanted to be upset at Harry for following her and for letting her believe that he did not know. Yet deep inside, she was glad that he already knew. She was now free of the burden of secrets. Harry knew everything about her, at least everything that she knew about herself. He had seen her naked soul, and he cherished her flaws. He knew everything and still wanted her. If that was not true love, nothing else could be.

CHAPTER XIV

***

Harry and Hope tied the knot a year after they had met at the hospital. Harry sold his flat in the city and moved into a cottage in the countryside with his stunning wife. Hope begged Catherine to move in with her and stay in their guest apartment but Catherine refused. She was too used to her lifestyle. She also did not want come between Hope and Harry in anyway, even as friend.

The rustic and cheap appearance of the outside of the cottage contrasted with its luxurious interior. The front double doors, made of cured mahogany, resembled the gates of heaven. They were a symbol of both safety and artistry. They opened up to a large fireplace at the center of the cottage. It was made of sets of smooth, exotic stones mounted on the wall, all the way up to the chimney. Right above the fireplace was a life-size portrait of Hope and Harry in their wedding clothes. They looked marvelous, powerful, domineering. Marble staircases ran throughout the three-story cottage, projecting ever-changing patterns on the ceiling at night.

The scintillating antique chandeliers and vintage furniture added character to the living room. That was where Harry kept a collection of lavish paintings. His great-grandfather was a German curator murdered by Nazis. His father and grandfather had both been great painters. Art was very important to Harry. He lacked the artistic talent bestowed upon his father and grandfather, so he always felt compelled to buy expensive paintings. Among his collection were *Portrait of Dr. Gachet* by Vincent van Gogh, *Saying Grace* by Norman Rockwell, and the very intriguing *Number 19* by Jackson Pollock. Harry also kept a thought-provoking hand-painted replica of Bouguereau's *La Nymphée* in the hallway. It was a gift from his late father.

The upstairs master bedroom had recently been renovated to add a new window opening on the southeast of the cottage. The window offered an awe-inspiring view of the Blue Basin Lake. Harry wanted to construct the perfect environment for his wife. The Blue Basin Lake was not as exotic as the infamous lake in the desert, but Harry tried his best to recreate Hope's most cherished memories.

Harry made Hope breakfast every morning before going to work. Every day was a day of celebration, with gifts and flowers. His love was suffocating at times, but Hope would not have it any other way. Harry endured a two-hour drive through winding

169

curves to make it to work every day. Yet he considered it a small sacrifice. His reward was the joy on Hope's face every time he came home after a busy day at work. He did not need any liquor or cigarettes to cope with the ghastly reality of a surgeon's life. Hope was his escape. She took pleasure in the simplest things. She enjoyed removing his tie, handing him a drink, and removing his shoes after he fell asleep on the couch.

Every Sunday, they stayed in bed until the late morning. They lightheartedly discussed everything ranging from politics to religion. They had divergent opinions on most things, but they rarely clashed. Their aptitude to be understanding and to empathize with each other was praiseworthy. In the midst of this semblance of perfection, the couple's first serious argument crept up on them one Sunday morning.

"Babe, have you heard about that crazy accident that happened on the freeway last night?" asked Hope, walking back into the bedroom with two cups of freshly brewed coffee.

"How could I, babe? I have been in bed with you all night long. You think I have mystical powers," joked Harry.

"Leave me, big head! I don't know, I was just asking. It's all over the news."

"What happened?"

"A minivan collided with a truck. It was pretty bad."

"Oh wow! This freeway is treacherous! Did anyone get hurt?" asked Harry.

"Yes, babe. There was a family of four in the van. The father and mother are in critical condition. Thank God the kids are okay," said Hope as she got back in bed and cuddled up to Harry.

"That's horrible! You never know what can happen. One day, you are happy and healthy; the next day, you are fighting for your life," said Harry pensively as he pulled Hope close to his chest and squeezed a bit.

"I know, right!" said Hope.

"I am not trying to be pushy or anything, but I think it's time we give it a shot, babe. I give you everything a woman could hope for. The only thing missing in our perfect picture is a child, Hope," grumbled Harry to Hope.

"I don't think I am ready for that yet, babe. We have talked about that. Can we give it some more time? It will happen soon. We don't need to rush."

"Soon? When is soon? You have been saying soon for the past six months!" exclaimed Harry.

"Soon is whenever my body feels ready, Harry. What has gotten into you? Putting pressure on me is not going to help. It will just make me more nervous. All I ask for is patience and understanding."

"I am a doctor, so don't you talk to me about your body not being ready. Your body is ready; I know it. I have been more than patient. You are dragging your feet; that's what it is. I am not fucking stupid, Hope."

"Dragging my feet for what, Harry? I am stuck with you! I don't plan on going anywhere, so why would I be dragging my feet? What do I need to buy time for? I am still traumatized by the thought of carrying a child. I am not ready mentally. You of all people should understand that. You know what I went through."

"You are stuck with me? That's how you think of me? Someone you are stuck with?"

"You know exactly what I meant, Harry. Don't twist my words and change the topic! You need to stop acting childish and understand where I am coming from."

"And you need to stop being a spoiled brat and start acting like the wife and mother I need you to be!"

"What? What does that even mean? How am I being a brat? The wife and mother you need me to be? Are you serious right now? You know what, enjoy your coffee, Harry. Enjoy your coffee," said Hope as she got up and left the room. She could not believe that Harry had stooped so low. She was deeply wounded by Harry's remarks, but she swallowed her tongue to prevent thrashing his ego.

Harry was consumed by the fear of aging. He wanted to enjoy the best years of his children before he grew old. He had seen firsthand what disease and the unpredictability of life could do to people. He had seen families broken by sudden strokes or heart attacks. He had seen kids' futures crumble due to unfortunate, silly accidents. He had seen motherless, fatherless kids trying to make sense of the disease that is cancer. He grew obsessed with the idea of being a father. He grew obsessed with the idea of being a good father. He grew obsessed with the fear of dying before seeing his kids succeed in life. He already had everything there was to have. His career was flourishing as he had recently been made head surgeon of the women's clinic where he'd met Hope. His estates were scattered across the country. He would never have to worry about his finances ever again. He was married to a woman who, despite all the shenanigans of life, was as exquisite as the morning bloom. The only thing missing in his life was a child, someone to channel all that energy into. A child was the ultimate motivation to strive for more. His life was becoming stagnant, and he refused to fall into the stillness of childless married life.

After a few days of ignoring each other, they mutually apologized. Hope knew that was the beginning of the end of her unsoiled happiness. She knew this topic was going to come up again and again. She was not against the idea of mothering Harry's children, but she wasn't ready for another pregnancy. She was still healing mentally from her miscarriage, and the simple thought of being with child gave her panic attacks.

Saturday, June 6, 2015 marked their one-year anniversary. It had only been two weeks since their first argument, and things were still a bit edgy. Hope was unsure about any anniversary activities. She expected Harry to make plans the night before but that never happened. Hope went to bed disappointed and concerned.

Hope was awakened at around eleven o'clock in the morning the following day by the sweet sound of Luther Vandross's "A House Is Not a Home." She walked into the living room and stood there in stupefaction. She counted at least four small- to

174

medium-sized gift boxes on top of the end table in the living room. On top of those boxes were two envelopes, red and white. Hope tiptoed between gift wrap and paperclips scattered across the living-room floor. She reached for the envelopes.

"Those aren't yours, lady," hollered Harry from across the room.

"They are mine now," said Hope as she proceeded to open the envelopes. The first envelope, the red one, contained two passes to a John Legend concert and a yearly pass to *SPA on the Sea*, one of the most luxurious spas in town. The second envelope contained two plane tickets to Ibiza, Portugal, leaving in seven hours.

"Harry! Oh my God! You are crazy!" exclaimed Hope in excitement. "I don't have clean clothes, and you know how long I take to pack. I am also going to need a bathing suit. Many bathing suits!" she screamed as she ran back into the bedroom and started looking for her suitcase. Harry followed her into the bedroom, pulled her toward himself, and kissed her.

"Who said anything about packing? Happy anniversary, babe! Now, get in the shower. We are leaving for the airport in an hour. I am sure Ibiza has shopping centers."

Hope was ecstatic. She couldn't believe that Harry had gone all out to make their anniversary memorable. Little did she know that Harry had ulterior motives. Behind that innocent, seemingly guileless face was an insidious, persistent man. Harry was obsessed with getting what he wanted, and he was not one to give up easily. The purpose of his trip to Ibiza was twofold. Harry was too proud to ask for forgiveness. The trip was his way of apologizing for pressing Hope. A spontaneous trip to the exotic Mediterranean island of Ibiza almost guaranteed Hope's clemency. The trip was also intended to get Hope to let her guard down. He connivingly planned a getaway on the paradisiac island of Ibiza. He knew that Hope's exhilaration almost guaranteed lapses in judgment that would result in Hope being pregnant.

The young couple had been on the island for six days; their getaway was coming to an end. Harry had accomplished all he had hoped to accomplish. He had been forgiven for his hurtful words, and his wife was glowing. On that last day, he stayed in bed until the late afternoon. He reminisced about an inebriated Hope wildly riding his stallion. He reminisced about her piercing screams of satisfaction. He reminisced about the numbing feeling on the tip of his phallus after he exploded inside of her time and time again. There was no doubt in Harry's mind that Hope was pregnant. He had been monitoring Hope's menstruation and had planned his trip accordingly.

Harry saw Hope standing on the private balcony in her purple satin lingerie. Such a marvelous sight awoke all his senses. She leaned on the hand rails, and her protruding posterior dared Harry to look away. She didn't notice Harry drooling. The wind drifted alongside the shore, and she lost herself in the depth of the cerulean sea. She felt grateful for Harry. She began to entertain the thought of having a child, the thought of carrying Harry's child. She was still very frightened, but the only way to overcome that fear was to face it. She would never be a hundred percent ready; she had to take a leap of faith. Harry was right; a child would be the final touch to her almost perfect life. Her decision was made; she would tell Harry about her willingness and her desire to bear his child as soon as they got back to the cottage. She turned around, and her smiling eyes met Harry's dreamy eyes.

"I am going to start packing up. Why don't you go ahead and order us something to eat?" said Harry.

"Lord knows you need food! I drained you, didn't I?" joked Hope.

"Correction. We need food! Don't act like you did not tap out this morning," said Harry.

They both laughed as Hope grabbed the phone to place an order. She often ordered twice the amount of food she could eat. In her mind, she was compensating for the times she'd had to ration her meals to make them last a full day. Harry watched her ordering food and grew impatient with her indecisiveness.

"Just pick one damn thing off the menu, Hope. It's really not that hard. You can never make up your mind," said Harry, as he opened up the closet door to get his shoes.

Hope rolled her eyes and gave him a dirty look. She ignored his little temper tantrum. It wasn't the first time Harry had spoken to her in such a demeaning manner. It was one of those things that Hope overlooked for the sake of love. She blamed it on Harry's upbringing.

Harry had been born into a wealthy family. His father was a painter turned lawyer. His mother was a sweet, loving lady who'd never worked a day in her life. She never had to. Harry's father provided amply for her. Harry was a brilliant, educated man born into a culture of bigotry, raised by and amid megalomaniacal sexists. From a very young age, he had been shielded from the reality of life. He was taught to be narcissistic. He found sexist jokes amusing. They were

"Good laughs for backyard bonfires," as his dad used to say. The marginalization of women was embedded in Harry's everyday life as a child and teenager. He grew up in this man-controlled environment and had been taught to be a controlling prick.

Their lunch arrived minutes after they finished packing. Hope had ordered Siamese steak for Harry but opted to try something new. She ordered a *sofrit pagès* for herself. Sofrit pagès was one of the island's specialties. It was a concoction of spicy pork, lamb, chicken, and various local vegetables and spices. It takes a cook with an exquisite artistic flair to mix three different types of meat into one dish. Hope looked at Harry's plate, and everything seemed bland and tasteless. She was transported into another world as soon as she removed the cover of her plate. The aroma was foreign yet familiar. It was a mixture of known and unknown smells of spices that tickled her nostrils. She inhaled a whiff of garlic and pepper that reminded her of her best days with Catherine. As she brought that spoon to her mouth, she was taken away by the savory taste of the meat—so creamy yet so misleadingly spicy.

Hope could not fully enjoy her food because she was being rushed by Harry. Their flight was leaving in a couple of hours. Harry would have enjoyed spending another night in Ibiza. It was the closest thing to paradise on earth. Yet he had serious meetings the

179

following day. He had meetings that even a man of his caliber did not have the luxury to postpone or cancel. They finished eating and gathered all their belongings. They made it to the airport in time to catch their flight, and Hope went to sleep only minutes after takeoff. She held Harry's hand tightly in her sleep. From the corner of his eye, Harry gawked at Hope sleeping on his shoulder. Her innocence and her beauty never ceased to amaze him. Even in her sleep, she awakened salacious thoughts in Harry's mind.

The soft voice of a stewardess woke Hope up from her sleep. The stewardess advised everyone to put on their seat belts and prepare for landing. The plane touched down smoothly, and the young couple disembarked the plane just as they'd boarded, holding hands and smiling. Harry was too tired to drive, and he wanted to enjoy the company of his wife. He had his chauffeur pick them up. Hope dozed off again on the way home. Harry was wide awake, enjoying the scenic view and the perfect ending to his trip.

Harry was forever worried about some impending doom. To him, there was no such thing as unending bliss. He was certain that glee was always temporary, always bound to end in discord. He had learned from experience that the feeling of exhilaration was often short-lived. He advised his chauffeur to be extra cautious. He was worried that an unfortunate event would come to tarnish his flawless night.

"Take it easy now, Jeff," he whispered to his driver, trying not to wake up Hope. "Turmoil is often impending every time happiness triumphs," he continued.

Jeff acquiesced with a nod of his head. Impending? What was Harry talking about? Jeff did not bother trying to make sense of his words. He just slowed down. They finally got home safely. Harry opened the car door and took a deep breath. He had missed the smell of orchids and lotuses characteristic of Hope's garden. He had overreacted as usual. There was no imminent danger, no mishap sent by the gods to disrupt his joy. They'd made it home safe and sound. He picked up Hope, still sleeping, and carried her all the way to her bedroom. She was deep asleep and drooled all over the pillow once Harry put her down. Harry looked around for a clean cloth to wipe off the trickle of drool. The bedroom was a mess with no clean cloth in sight.

Harry noticed Hope's purse on the bed next to her and opened it up, looking for napkins. He went through her purse, and his facial expression shifted from jovial to baleful. His dreams shattered as he laid eyes on the birth-control pills sitting at the bottom of Hope's purse. He retired into the bathroom and closed the door behind him. He sat on the toilet lid, holding his head with both hands. He looked as if he had seen the devil himself.

The devil himself—intriguing expression, isn't it? Such a trivial and universal saying used by so many great poets and romancers with a knack for devilish things. *The devil himself.* Is it then being argued that all evil principles are inherently masculine? Such premise does not appear to be far-fetched but it's probably better to focus our attention on Harry's anger-inducing predicament.

His eyes were bloodshot; his nostrils flared like those of a jaguar about to pounce. He took notice of his closed fist and released it quickly. His much-anticipated prospect of pregnancy vanished in front of his eyes. His most cherished dream turned into an unending nightmarish shamble. There's no worse feeling for a con artist than to be conned. Harry had hoped to selfishly trick Hope into having his child, but karma toyed with his plans. Deep inside, he wanted to set the room ablaze. Hope had no malicious intent when she began taking birth-control pills, but Harry felt played, misled. It was almost as if someone were standing on his chest, causing his rib cage to crush his heart.

CHAPTER XV

***

Harry snatched the pills out of the bag and walked out of the bathroom. He coasted past Hope sleeping and vehemently slammed the windows shut. Hope jumped up and looked around in a frantic manner. Her confused eyes met Harry's anger. He stood by the bed and stared her down with disdain in his eyes.

"Can you explain to me what the fuck that is?" he uttered ragingly as he catapulted the pills at Hope. His menacing tone left her aghast. She picked up the birth-control pills and threw them onto the nightstand.

"They are obviously birth-control pills, Harry. What has gotten into you? Why are you raising your voice at me and throwing shit at me?"

"Where the fuck did you get them?" said Harry, furious.

"Catherine gave them to me, but that's beside the damn point, though. Why are you throwing a fit over birth-control pills?"

184

"It never occurred to you to consult me first before you started taking these stupid pills?"

"Consult you? As in 'ask for your permission'? To take birth-control pills? Listen to yourself, Harry. Did you consult me first before you went snooping in my purse?"

"Do not try to change the topic, or I swear to God, Hope, you are not going to like the way this conversation ends. As your husband, I have a right to know when you are on birth control."

"Are you threatening me right now? You need to calm yourself down, Harry. They are just birth-control pills, for Christ's sake. You are acting like you found out I cheated. Did I not tell you that I was not ready yet for a pregnancy? How did you think I was going to prevent that from happening? You take so much pleasure in spilling your semen inside of me every chance you get. You thought I was going to sit there and hope I don't get pregnant?"

"Watch your condescending tone, Hope, before I remove that snake tongue of yours from your mouth. Typical! Treacherous! You knew I wanted children, and you deceived me by ingurgitating pills behind my back."

"I deceived you? How? By trying to protect myself. And why would you still try to impregnate me after I told you I was not ready? And I am the treacherous one? That is so devious of you and so beneath you. You broke my heart, Harry."

Harry had inadvertently showed his true colors to Hope. In the heat of the argument, he confessed his deceitful intentions to impregnate Hope. He stormed out of the room, mumbling under his breath, and left a distraught Hope wondering what had just happened. Hope expected Harry, of all people, to understand and support her choices. She did not know how to react to such an alarming display of perfidious behavior. For an instant, she feared for her safety. She understood Harry's frustration and desire to be a father, but there was no excuse to act the way he did. Harry was inconsiderate and selfish, to say the least.

This argument should have been Hope's cue to start planning a life without Harry, but she missed it. Once again, she ignored the signs. She ignored the red flags waving in her face, blinded by a desire to make things work. She was tired of failing at things and was determined to salvage her marriage. To her, it was just an isolated incident. The threats and the violence in Harry's voice made Hope uneasy, but she was even more upset that Harry's impatience had ruined it all.

She no longer felt okay with carrying his child. His temper turned her off.

Hope refused to embark once again on a journey that she was not ready for. She understood that the concept of compromise was at the very core of all relationships, whether it be of a sexual, romantic, or economic nature. There are things in life that most people are willing to sacrifice for the sake of happiness. And then there are things intrinsic to one's wholeness and personality; things that cannot be overlooked or compromised on. Some women have sacrificed everything and anything to please the vainest desires of their spouses. Hope was not one of these women. She was all for compromising, but she needed Harry to meet her halfway. Getting pregnant to please Harry was not a mere compromise to her; it was self-destruction. She refused to self-destruct. She spent days thinking about the conundrum she faced.

Many weeks went by before Hope and Harry uttered a word to each other. Harry, who was usually very loquacious, was quiet like a mime when Hope was around. It was almost as if he had taken a vow of silence. He moved all his belongings into the guest room. Hope struggled every night to fall asleep. She was so used to having the warmth of Harry on her back. Every night, she held onto Harry's pillows and placed them between her legs to create the illusion of being held tightly. The emptiness of her bedroom was driving her mad. She knew she was not to blame, but she felt compelled to try to fix things. She refused to believe that Harry was just another controlling and misogynistic fraud of a man. She wanted to make things right; she just did not know how to.

Harry was also filled with doubts, anger, and remorse. He was torn between the need to make things right and his pressing, growing desire to have a child. Hope was only fifty feet away, in the next room, but Harry already felt the void left by her absence. He did not want to lose her; she had been the core of his existence for the past three years. Blinded by pride and consumed by guilt, he failed to realize the toll the situation was taking on his marriage. He tried to drown his loneliness in whisky, but the elixir of the gods provided only a momentary escape. Time drove a wedge between the young couple. Harry's ego grew bigger by the day. He started coming home very late from work; rare were the nights when he came home sober.

Hope could hear him every night, sneaking into the house as quiet as a drunk man can be. Night after night, she stayed in bed with her eyes wide open, waiting for Harry to come home, staring at the ceiling, watching her marriage slowly sink into this infinite dark hole.

After what seemed to be an eternity, Hope decided to be the bigger person and initiate a much-needed conversation. Yes, it was derisory that Harry felt disrespected, considering he was the one being loud, distant, and obnoxious. Hope overlooked it all for the sake of her marriage. She hoped to save her marriage, and the only way to do so was to sacrifice a bit of her pride. She woke up early that Sunday and cooked breakfast for two—scrambled eggs, bacon, orange juice, and French toast. She then sat in the kitchen and waited for Harry to come get his daily newspapers.

"Harry. We should talk, honey. Let's eat breakfast and talk," murmured Hope as Harry walked into the kitchen.

"Oh, you think we should talk? Well, let's talk then. What should we talk about?"

"Can you stop being cold and sarcastic? I am trying, here. This is not all on me. I am not the one who moved into the guest room."

"Here you go again with the pointing fingers. Yes, Hope, this is all your doing. I am not being sarcastic at all. So once again, what would you like to talk about?"

"Many things, including the future of our marriage. We can't keep going on like this. We used to be a team, Harry. What can we do to get back to that?"

"Yes, we used to be a team, a team in which I do all the hard work and you collect the benefits. You want to know what you can do to make this work? I will tell you. Get pregnant and give me a son, then we will work on our marriage," said Harry dismissively.

"There you go again with the ultimatums. Why don't you try to understand my position, Harry? A child is not a bargaining chip. Why are you doing this to me? Why are you knowingly putting me in an impossible situation?" complained Hope. The sadness in her voice would have touched the coldest of men.

"It's not an impossible situation. You need to stop being stubborn and difficult. You are not the only woman in the world."

"Harry, your words poke holes in my heart every time you speak so harshly. I know you have been seeing someone. I am not stupid. I can't prove it, but I can feel it in my guts. I want us to start over, full disclosure and fresh start. Can we try that?"

"Start over and then do what? Act like you never disrespected me by taking pills behind my back?"

"Harry! You need to stop shifting the blame and let that shit go. What do you want me to say? You know what? Here it goes. I apologize for not asking for your permission, Harry. I am not ready for a child right now, so is it okay with you if I take birth-control pills for a little while longer?" said Hope in an acerbic tone.

"Do as you please. You are already taking them anyways. I guess I will have to wait until you are ready, then," replied Harry as he left the room. He wanted to end the conversation; his mind was elsewhere. His voice lacked sincerity and left Hope unconvinced, but she still held onto a thread of hope.

As is often the case with marriages and relationships, something dies with every argument. Trust was broken. Hope knew Harry was seeing someone else. She had no actual proof, but her gut feelings had never lied to her before.

There was an overly apprehensive man camouflaged behind this educated, cultivated persona that Harry portrayed. He was threatened by Hope's natural wit. His manhood was imperiled. He needed a docile housewife, someone content in domesticity. He needed someone to stroke his ego on demand. Hope was not that person. He realized that she was not going to allow him to walk all over her. He realized that she was going to put up a fight. The lack of aggressiveness in her action made her even more threatening to Harry. He feared Hope's ability to remain fairly calm even when he pushed her buttons.

Harry barely spoke to Hope, and when he did, it was to complain, nag, and harshly criticize. After weeks of agonizing mistreatment and verbal abuse, Hope asked Catherine to accompany her to church. She was not a fervent believer, but she needed a safe outlet to socialize and vent a bit. That Sunday, Catherine stopped by, against her better judgment, to pick up Hope. She waited for Hope in the living room for forty-five minutes. She sat on the long sofa facing the window, staring at the floor. On one chair was Enoch, the house cat. On the adjacent chair was Harry, watching the television with his headphones on. He tried his best to ignore the very existence of Catherine.

Finally, Hope emerged from the bedroom, unrecognizable. Her protruding hips greeted the embracing texture of her obsidian-black dress. Her slender eyebrows touched as she glanced at Harry from the second floor. She wanted to see his reaction. He was too lost in his show to notice Hope. Catherine was the first to see her coming down the stairs. She anchored her eyes on Hope's high-heeled shoes for a few seconds. They were marvelous.

"Oh my God, Hope! You are ravishing," she screamed in an upsurge of excitement. Hope acknowledged her compliment with a subtle smile that exposed her pearly teeth.

"How do I look, hon?" said Hope as she moved in front of Harry, placing herself between him and the television. Harry glanced at her in a disinterested way.

"You look fine!" he replied, waving her off rudely.

No. She did not look fine. She looked exquisite. She looked stunning. She looked divine. And even those weak words did not accurately describe how she looked. Her beauty was beyond the realm of what words can describe. She was disappointed by the dry and forced compliment coming from her husband. She was not the only one to notice Harry's total disinterest. Catherine did as well, and she immediately knew there was serious trouble in paradise. Hope begged her not to ask any questions. Despite her inquisitive nature, Catherine understood that some topics were better left alone. They spent the entire morning at church. They gossiped more than they worshipped. They ate brunch after church and reminisced about their time together. They laughed at the life-changing experiences they had shared. Hope refrained from mentioning the constant fights with Harry because she did not want Catherine to worry about her. She returned home in the early afternoon to find Harry still on the couch.

"What's for dinner?" asked Harry as soon as she walked in.

"I don't know, Harry. I am not hungry. Catherine and I already ate."

"Oh, I see. It must have felt great leaving your husband starving at home and using his money to feed your leech of a friend."

"Harry, grow up!" shouted Hope as she retreated to her bedroom and locked the door behind her.

It became evident to Hope that things could no longer be fixed. This marriage was doomed after all. Harry was draining; his insecurities were running rampant. Hope was the only one trying to work things out, and it was getting exhausting. It was time for her to start doing things for herself. It was time to find a job, get an education, and do whatever it took to become self-reliant and self-sufficient.

CHAPTER XVI

Hope considered asking the women in her community for advice and guidance. But what advice could they possibly give her? They would probably tell her to be submissive and to stop complaining. They were all seemingly content with their mediocre lives. Hope observed them daily whether it was at the nearby park, in their backyards, or during public gatherings. She was baffled by their ability to be completely selfless in an idiotic kind of way. They nonchalantly sacrificed their dignity and their freedom. They were deprived of the right to an opinion, but they never complained. Their husbands' words were gospel to their ears—a bunch of puppets and puppeteers in a big old circus. She pitied these women trapped in this semblance of happiness. She pitied their daughters being raised in this modernized cult of domesticity.

The only difference between Hope and all these happy-go-lucky women was of a monetary nature. They all came from wealthy families. Every single one of them could have easily divorced her fraud of a husband and still been just fine. Hope could not comprehend why they chose to stay and be the marionettes of unscrupulous men. Was it the fear of being alone forever, or maybe the fear of being judged by their peers? They seemed so concerned about maintaining a certain status quo, concerned enough to sacrifice their personal happiness for an apparent togetherness. They could never survive the void that a divorce would leave because they lived to please their folks and impress their peers.

Harry's money was Hope's shackles; her options were limited. She cared very little about status quo; she had no peers nor folks to impress. She now faced the same dilemma she had faced at the tavern after her suicide attempt: pack up and leave without a plan or suck it up until she came up with a plan. She opted for the latter option. If homelessness had taught her one thing, it was not to act impulsively. She could not stand being on the street again; she would not allow herself to become a burden to Catherine once again. The best course of action was to prepare herself for the storm to come.

Hope had developed a keen interest in nursing — mainly due to her experiences at the clinic. So she decided to enroll in nursing school. She had to give herself something to fall back on if worse came to worst. She waited until Harry left for work and went into town with Catherine to register for classes. They spent the day filling out paperwork and going through unnecessary orientations. She tried to get back home before sundown. She hoped to make it home before Harry; she did not want to have to explain her whereabouts. To her great surprise, she walked in on Harry watching television. For some odd reason, he had left work early that day. He was sitting on the sofa with his feet up, drinking a bottle of aged whisky that he had sworn to never open.

"Hey, Harry," whispered Hope as she walked past him.

"Where the fuck were you, Hope? I have been home for almost an hour now. The house is a mess, and you are out doing God knows what with God knows whom."

"Harry, please don't start. I went into town with Catherine."

"Catherine! Always Catherine. How many times have I told you that I don't like that friendship? I don't want that friendship."

"Harry, I am not in the mood to argue right now," she said as she walked away.

"Don't you dare walk away from me when I am talking to you!"

"You are not talking to me. You are scolding me like I am your child. Catherine is all I have in this world, so no, I am not going to end my friendship because you decide to get drunk and talk nasty to me."

"Yes, you will end this friendship, Hope. You will end it, or I will end it for you. She is a dirty and depraved destitute who only sticks around because you are paying for her shit. Well, because I am paying for her shit."

"Harry, I was a 'dirty and depraved destitute' too when you started courting me. I was in the same boat as Catherine. That did not seem to bother you then. Why is our friendship bothering you now?"

"Yes, you were a dirty and depraved destitute! And you should be grateful that I made you who you are now. You should show gratitude to the man who made a respectable woman out of you. You should show your gratitude by doing what I ask you to do when I ask you to do it."

"Fuck you, Harry. You made me a respectable woman, yet you disrespect me every chance you get. Who am I respectable to if not to my own husband?"

"No, fuck you. You brought the disrespect on yourself. You disrespected my home by bringing your filthy whore of a friend in here every chance you get.

You disrespected me when you decided that I was not worthy enough to father your child. I took you in. I disregarded the fact that you had been nothing but a tavern prostitute who didn't even know the father of her child. I took you in. You repaid me with blatant disrespect."

"Harry, you are hurting me right now, and I don't know why. What have I done to you to deserve such treatment? You need to stop."

"No. You need to stop talking to me like I am the typical thug down the street. I know that's what you are used to. Sometimes I ask myself if you were really raped. Maybe you enjoyed having those thugs inside of you."

Hope did not know how to respond to that. It was unclear to her how Harry had found out about the rape. The women at the clinic must have been gossiping about her. Harry had stooped so low that there was no coming back from this point. He had thrown Hope's past in her face in the cruelest way possible, and her heart was aching. She had been hurt time and time again by all kinds of people. She had never heard more stabbing words coming from someone pretending to love her. Her eyes became glassy as she fought back tears. The last thing she wanted was to give Harry the satisfaction of seeing her broken. She stood there with her glassy piercing blue eyes and stared down the devil that had risen in Harry. A deadly stillness hovered over them. Harry stood up, grabbed his bottle of whisky, and waddled into the bedroom.

As soon as the bedroom door closed, Hope dropped to her knees, incapable of holding her emotions any longer. She did not shed a single tear. The real pain was inside of her chest. She felt her heart being ripped into pieces. She held onto the carpet as an attempt to transfer that anger. She lay on the couch and fell asleep. When she woke up the following morning, Harry had already left for work. She was glad. She did not know how she was going to interact with him moving forward. She knew Harry was going to apologize, buy flowers, and plan a few trips. She knew he was going to try to buy her forgiveness. Harry was one of those men who thought money was the answer to everything. No amount of money could restore the damage he had caused to Hope's confidence. Hope called Catherine as soon as she finished eating breakfast.

"Hey, Hope. I was just about to call you. How are you doing, baby girl?"

"I am doing okay. Just home bored, as usual."

"Are you sure you are okay? Your voice sounds muffled. Somebody is getting a cold, huh?"

"No, Cathy. I wish I was getting a cold. It's much worse, to be honest. Harry is out of control."

"Oh God! What did he do?"

"What hasn't he done? Yesterday after I left you, I got home and found him on the couch. He cursed at me, called me all types of names. He called you all types of names. I am scared, Cathy. I think he might get violent eventually. All he does is drink and belittle me. You couldn't imagine the things he said to me, Cathy—despicable things, things I could not dare to repeat to you. I am also certain he is cheating on me."

"Oh God, baby! I am so sorry to hear that. I knew something was wrong. I knew you were not happy; I could feel it. You did not want to talk about it, so I left it alone. He is toxic! Who would have thought he would be such an asshole? What are you going to do?" said Catherine in an almost-panicking voice.

"I do not know, Cathy. I need to think. He left early this morning. I know he's going to buy me the world to forgive him, but he went too far this time."

"This time? That has happened before? Hope, why am I just now hearing about all of this?"

"Yeah. He found out that I was taking the pills you gave me, and he almost had a heart attack. Things have been spinning out of control since then. That's insane."

"Hope, you have got to leave him. He sounds like a controlling freak. He is not going to change. I am here for you. You know that, right? You have got to leave before it's too late."

"Leave to go where, Cathy? You don't work anymore. I don't have a job. I don't think I can go back to living under that bridge. I worry every night, knowing you are still out there on your own."

"Well, I don't know. Isn't it better than losing your mind? Who knows what he is going to say or do the next time he decides to get drunk?"

"There has to be a better way. I must find a better way, Cathy. If I can prove that he has been abusive, then I can get a divorce."

"Be careful, hon. He is not going to count his losses and let you leave with half of his money."

"I don't care about his money, Cathy. I just want peace."

"I will come by in a few hours and stay with you, okay? You don't sound right."

"No, Cathy. He hates you! I don't want you to be subjected to his disgusting mouth. If he finds you here, that will set him off."

"Oh God. I don't like this, Hope. Anyways, I will see you Sunday. Call me if he tries anything funny, okay?"

Hope hung up the phone and jumped in the shower to wash the sadness off her face. Harry was about to be home anytime. She wanted to look strong and unwavering, ready to turn down apologies and gifts. She didn't know yet how she was going to get out of this marriage. She knew, though, that the broken pieces of her heart could never be put back together, at least not by Harry. She was willing to endure his presence for a little while longer until she finished her nursing courses and secured a job.

She had just finished taking a shower when Harry pulled into the driveway. He walked past her as if she were invisible and locked the guest bedroom's door behind him. There were no gifts, no flowers, and no apologies.

Hope was relieved that she did not have to address him at all that night. They avoided each other for days. That Saturday morning, Hope woke early to get ready for her first class. She was in her underwear, fixing her makeup, when Harry walked into her bedroom. She knew it was not a friendly visit. The scheming, devilish look in his eyes betrayed his soft and sarcastic voice.

"Looking lovely," he said as he closed the door behind him. The stench of whisky invaded the room as soon as Harry opened his mouth. Hope was too familiar with that smell. It brought back the ugliest of memories to her mind.

"Harry, it is only nine o'clock in the morning, and you are already drunk. You are pathetic," said Hope.

"I am not drunk. You smell great, my love. Getting pretty for me?" said Harry. He cornered Hope between the wall and the dresser and wrapped his arms around her. Hope's senses spiked.

"Let go of me. Fuck off, Harry!" yelled Hope, trying to wiggle free.

"Come on, babe. You know you crave my touch."

"Actually, I do not, and you are scaring me right now. I've got to go to class, so let go of me."

"Class? You are in school now? When were you planning on telling me?" said Harry, letting go of Hope just a little.

"Never. My schooling has nothing to do with you. Get the fuck off me. You are hurting me!" screamed Hope as she pushed him vigorously and broke free. She ran into the bathroom with her cell phone and locked herself in. She called the police and got into the bathtub, curled up behind the shower curtain. She no longer controlled her actions at this point; fear had taken over her body. Her heart accelerated every time Harry punched the door and ordered her to open it.

"Open up, whore," he said again and again. "Open up, or I will break the fucking door down. You are my wife, this is my home, and you will do as I say."

Hope hoped that the door held a little longer until the police arrived. Hell-bent on getting to Hope, Harry grabbed the knob with his left hand and thrust his shoulder against the door repeatedly. He slammed his whole body against the door like a raging bull. The door slowly began to succumb to the repeated slamming and banging. Harry was seconds from unhinging the door from its frame when an Ashbourne City Police Department patrol car pulled into the driveway. The sirens brought Harry back to his senses; he stopped banging on the door.

CHAPTER XVII

***

"ACPD. Please open the door."

Harry's footsteps walked away from the bathroom door, toward the front door. Hope waited a few minutes then opened the bathroom door. She peeped down the hallway to make sure Harry was gone. She ran toward the blinking lights of the police car. As she pushed the front door open, she saw something that numbed her legs. Harry was already outside, joking and laughing with the police officers. They did not appear concerned about Hope's safety. At that moment, she realized how embroiled she really was in Harry's web. She refused to believe that even the police were on Harry's side. She knew Harry was a man of influence. She did not know about his hefty grants to the local police station and his long-standing friendship with the police chief. She wiped her eyes dry walked out to confront Harry in front of the police. Before she had a chance to open her mouth, one of the officers approached her with a hand on his service weapon.

"Hi there, Mrs. Huntelaard. Is everything okay? Harry told us that you have been acting a bit hysterical. He says he has it under control now."

"I have been acting hysterical? Are you kidding me? I called you, okay? I called you, not him. He tried to force himself on me, so I called you!" screamed Hope.

"Ma'am, we are going to need you to calm down. Out of respect for your husband, we would rather solve this in an amiable fashion. You are being disorderly right now. We know you have a mental ailment, but that is no excuse to act a fool."

"Are you fucking kidding me? A mental ailment? What mental ailment? He attacked me, you pig. I called you! Why would I call the police on myself?"

Hope had lost her cool. She realized her that the police officers were not going to be of any help. Her anger overflowed, and her choice of words deeply unsettled the police officers. She was in handcuffs before she could blink. Harry stood there with a smirk on his face, enjoying the embarrassment he had caused her once more.

Hope spent the night in a jail cell, staring at a stained wall. She was outraged by the turn of events, but she found some satisfaction in being locked away from Harry. It was a sad consolation that a jail cell was safer than the comfort of her own home. She stayed awake all night, unable to fall asleep. Every time she tried to close her eyes, the image of Harry's hands crawling up her dress came to haunt her dreams. At eight o'clock in the morning, a young lady finally came to get her out of her cell. She was in her early twenties. Her shiny, crisp, well-maintained uniform and her glossy leather belt suggested that she was new to the force.

"You are very lucky," she said. "Usually, you have to wait until Monday to see a judge if you get arrested over the weekend."

Hope ignored her. She did not feel lucky one bit; she knew who was pulling the strings to get her out of jail, and she knew it was not in good faith. Hope was escorted back home by two police cars.

Harry opened the door and greeted the police officers with coffee and donuts. He was more jovial than ever and surprisingly sober. He was in a cheerful mood. His talkative personality seemed to have returned. He had slept his drunkenness away and had forgotten— or pretended to have forgotten—what had happened the night before. They went inside and left an anxious Hope in the back seat of the patrol car. Half an hour later, they emerged from the house, laughing. Hope watched them talk on the front porch for another hour or so.

Eventually, the short bald-headed officer pointed at the car, and they all laughed at something Harry said. They walked up to the passenger-side door; one officer held the door open as another one reached in to grab Hope's arms. She pushed his hand and moved away from the open door. She did not want to go back to a house where the devil had set up camp. They managed to get her out of the car without too much trouble. They waved goodbye to Harry as he walked her inside of the house.

Hope was broken, passive and docile. She went up the steps quietly. There was no point in fighting. The police did not believe her story. Any attempt to resist would only add fuel to the fire and confirm the rumor that she was mentally ill. She'd had time to think in the back of the police car, and she knew the only way out of this situation was to divorce Harry. She also knew that it had to be done without raising any suspicion.

Harry had the ability to be simultaneously charming and cruel. He displayed a sociopathic duplicity that allowed a monster to thrive behind his angel's face, a sociopathic duplicity that allowed angels and demons to cohabitate within his soul in the most harmonious way possible. He showed no sign of remorse as he proceeded to make Hope's life a living hell. He forbade her to take any more classes and even had her followed by a private eye. She lived in a constant state of fear, always worried about Harry coming home intoxicated. From her bedroom window, she watched a black Buick with tinted windows drive up and around the house every day. The car then parked down the street, feet away from the entrance gate. She knew she was being watched. She had not talked to Catherine for days, and she never left the house. She began to lose any notion of time because her bedroom was always dark, regardless of the time of the day. Her paranoia intensified with each day that went by. Her health deteriorated quickly.

Harry took a sadistic pleasure in seeing her suffer. He was too far gone. He cared more about feeding his ego than he cared about Hope. He needed to see her broken to feel powerful again. He needed to torture her mentally and emotionally to regain control. His verbal outbursts and abuse became more and more common. He never missed an occasion to lash out at her. Hope became immune to the piercing pain caused by his elaborate insults.

It had been two months since Catherine and Hope talked. Catherine feared the worst; it was not like Hope to never reach out and check on her. She tried her best to stay out of her marriage. Her instincts told her that something had gone horribly wrong. Hope stopped responding to her messages. Every time she called the house phone, the call either went to voice mail or was picked up by Harry. She was disgusted by the way Harry was treating her friend. She blamed herself for not seeing through his lies. She could have prevented it all if she had not been so distracted. She couldn't even blame Hope for missing the red flags because she had missed them herself. She should have known that Harry was not a naively charming doctor. Harry was a sociopathic sack of excremental waste. She decided to make the trip to Hope's house and check up on her.

Thursdays were the busiest day around town. Tourists flooded the downtown streets, creating a chaotic maze and slowing down traffic. Thursdays were also the busiest days at the hospital. That was the only day Catherine was certain that Harry would not be home. She took two buses and a long cab ride to make it to Hope's house. Catherine arrived at Hope's house at around eleven in the morning. A rush of adrenaline spurted through her blood-filled veins as she walked past Harry's black limousine. After unfruitfully ringing the bell many times, she turned the knob. To her great surprise, the front door had been left unlocked; it made a subtle creaking noise as Catherine pushed it open.

Catherine felt as though she were entering one of those haunted castles described in morbid novels. The living room's curtains were closed, and all the lights were off. What was she going to do if she found herself face to face with Harry in the middle of this somber room? What would he do to her if he found her creeping inside of his home? Harry hated her with a passion. She dreaded the daunting outcome of any scenario where Harry caught her in his living room, yet her trembling legs were not going to impinge on her resolve to see Hope. She walked through the living room, knocking a few things down in the process. She tiptoed up the stairs and waddled her way to Hope's bedroom. She peeked through the cracked-open door of Hope's bedroom.

"Oh my God," gasped Catherine in disbelief. Her muscles weakened as she looked at a disfigured and alarmingly thin Hope lying in her bed, eyes wide open, staring at the ceiling. The shocking contrast between the large king-sized bed and the frail body of Hope freaked her out.

"Who's out there?" shrieked Hope at the top of her lungs. She jumped out of the bed, slid behind her dresser, and grabbed the night lamp lying on the floor.

"It's me, Hope. It's Cathy," said Catherine.

She opened the door and turned on the light. The bedroom looked both repulsive and sad. The rancid smell of stale dishes and rotten banana peels irritated Catherine's nostrils as soon as she walked into the room. As she approached the bedroom, a foul urinelike odor welcomed her. The whole room was a mixture of foul scents. Catherine threw up twice as she attempted to talk to Hope. The floor was completely covered with dirty clothing and stained bedsheets. The texture of the air was heavy, suggesting that the windows had not been opened for days, even weeks. A large number of motes floated in the air and rushed in the direction of the open door.

"Turn off the lights, Catherine. Turn off the damn lights. They are burning my eyes."

"Hope! Shut up. Just shut up already! Don't say another word right now. And leave the lights on, for Christ's sake!" yelled Catherine, disconcerted. She couldn't make sense of the situation Hope had found herself in. She had never seen such a worrisome state of despondency in her twenty-three years living in the streets. She turned around and tried to make eye contact with Hope. She needed an explanation. She saw Hope curled up behind the dresser, muttering inaudible words. She approached Hope. Her heart skipped several beats once she finally heard what Hope was saying.

"Don't yell at me, don't yell at me, don't yell at me," Hope kept repeating. "Why do you all keep yelling at me? Please don't yell at me. Cathy, please don't yell at me. Not you too."

Catherine did not mean to yell at her. She was shocked and upset that Hope had allowed herself to fall into such a dark hole. She was mad at herself for waiting so long to come and check on her best friend, her only friend.

"I am so sorry, Hope. I didn't mean to yell at you. Come on, hon. Come out from under there. Let's get you cleaned up."

She pulled Hope up by her shoulders and walked her to the bathroom. Hope's eyes were glassy. She looked up at Catherine and stared for a while, but her face was deprived of emotion; it was just a blank, confused stare. Catherine turned on the water and sat Hope in the bathtub with her clothes on. She filled up the tub halfway and let Hope soak for a while. Catherine then returned to the bedroom wearing an improvised face mask made from a pillow case. It took her two and a half hours to finally make the room livable again. By the time she was done, she had two heavy bags of filthy, stinking dirty clothes that needed to be thrown out. She returned to the bathroom to find Hope asleep in the bathtub.

Catherine wetted Hope's face gently to wake her up. She then rubbed her from head to toe with a lavender-scented shower gel. As she was walking her back to the bedroom, Hope grabbed the back of

216

Catherine's head and laid a kiss on her right cheek. Not one word was exchanged, but Catherine understood the meaning of that kiss. It was a thank-you kiss. It was a tender kiss that screamed, *"Thank you for being there for me, always and forever. Thank you for always showing up when least expected and always delivering on the promise to be my rock. Thank you for being family, thank you for being my friend, thank you for being Mom, and thank you for being you."* Catherine smiled a little. She put Hope back to bed and cracked the window open to let some light and fresh air in.

"Don't move, okay? You need to eat. I am going to get you something really quick."

Catherine made her a smoothie with a bacon sandwich. When she got back to the bedroom, Hope was deep asleep, snoring. She pulled up a seat and sat right next to her. She held her hand tightly, and that immense sensation of déjà vu took over her senses. She wanted to lay her head on the edge of the bed and rest her eyes. She recalled that night at the hospital. She recalled dozing off, holding Hope's hands; she recalled being awakened by the then-suave Harry. The thought of waking up to Harry standing over her kept her from falling asleep. She kept her eyes peeled and her ears open. Hope slept for three hours. It was already six o'clock in the evening when she woke up. She devoured her sandwich as though she had not eaten in days. She turned around to thank

Catherine, but her eyes came across the clock on the wall.

"What are you still doing here, Cathy? Harry is going to be home anytime now. He is going to kill you if he finds you in here."

"I am not leaving you here, Hope. You are coming with me. This man is going to destroy you. Look at you! You look like we haven't seen each other in twenty years. You are all wrinkled up. Your eyes are buried in their sockets, and your cheekbones…! Let's not even talk about your cheekbones. I thought you were dead when I first laid eyes on you, Hope!" Catherine's words were not pleasant. They were meant to be a wakeup call to Hope. Catherine spoke from the heart; she was never one to sugarcoat her feelings. She had always been passionate about the things she cared for. If there was one thing she truly cared about in this world, it was Hope.

"I know, Catherine. Don't you think I know that? I am lost. He screams at me every day. He says awful things to me, nasty things. Sometimes when he is screaming at me, I wish to die. I wish he was punching me repeatedly in my face instead. The pain and suffering from within is more dreadful than any physical pain. He took away my keys. I call the police on him; they come here, have drinks, and discuss football. He disconnects the phone in my bedroom when he leaves the house. He doesn't even bother coming upstairs to talk to me. He screams his insults from the first floor and waits until he hears me cry to stop," explained Hope.

"He needs to rot in hell. That's why I said you are coming with me, Hope. I will not leave this house without you."

"Cathy, this is not possible. Here, come. Look through the window. The house is being watched twenty-four, seven, Cathy. I am living in that infernal hole where I am constantly burning but can never die," sobbed Hope.

Catherine looked through the window and noticed the black car parked at the cross street.

"Are you serious? This is insane," said Catherine. "We have got to do something, Hope. You are in prison. There has to be something we can do to put an end to this revolting farce."

"I need to get a divorce, but he is friends with every lawyer around here. I need to build a case and prove that he is a threat to my health and safety. I don't know how to go about it."

"I can take care of all that for you downtown. I know a lawyer friend. He owes me a favor. Harry will never know anything until he gets the divorce papers. By then, it will be too late."

"That sounds like a great plan. But aren't they going to request my presence?"

"I have my ways, Hope. Avoid him for at least another six weeks or so. I will get you out of here. I promise."

Catherine's word was all Hope needed for now; she knew Catherine always kept her promises. They planned Hope's freedom meticulously; there was no room for mistakes. Catherine understood how unsafe it was to visit. They decided to communicate via emails. As Catherine left the house, she walked inches away from the parked car. She wanted to have a good look at the investigator—or goon—that was watching Hope. Unfortunately, the windows were heavily tinted. Her heart raced as she walked away from the car. She was disappointed that she did not get to see the face of the driver, but she was also glad that he did not step out to confront her.

Catherine wasted no time. Time was critical. Every minute Hope spent inside of that house was a minute Catherine would have to spend worrying about her. She was determined to file for divorce on behalf of Hope as soon as possible. Claims for divorce were to include accusations of domestic violence, sexual misconduct, substance abuse, and neglect.

CHAPTER XVIII

***

The light at the end of the tunnel is what motivates people to take those few final strides toward the end of a dreadful journey. The sight of the finish line always motivates the marathoner to gather all the strength left in his tired legs.

Hope found some sense of relief in the fact that Catherine knew of her desperate situation. Only a few weeks ago, she was standing at the very edge of an infinite abyss. She had accepted this bottomless pit of desolation as her final dwelling. Catherine showed up and gave her something to look forward to. Catherine gave her hope. She could now see the light at the end of her tunnel of misery.

Catherine tried her best to keep Hope updated on the progress of the divorce proceedings. Catherine was in contact of a lawyer friend she had met at The Concord and they were working on strategies to guarantee a swift divorce.

Hope was grateful for everything Catherine had done for her and continued to do for her. She knew Catherine did not expect any payback. There were no favors owed, yet she swore to repay Catherine some way, somehow. She had never been with Harry because of his money; she had never been interested in pompous dresses and fancy cars. She married him because he made her feel safe and wanted, desired and cared for. Yet she understood that the only good thing that could come out of this dysfunctional man was a divorce settlement, a breath of fresh air, and some financial stability to start anew.

Hope started daydreaming about her future life, her life without Harry. She started daydreaming about the things she would accomplish with a divorce settlement. She would buy Catherine a nice little house in the countryside—a nice little house with a front porch and a little garden. Catherine could grow asparagus and tomatoes on one side, spices on the other side… or flowers. Flowers would be nice. Catherine could sit on her porch every evening and read as many feminist books as her eyes would allow her to read. She could have a nice little library filled with books that she would never get to read, filled with books that she'd already read but would like to read again: Virginia Woolf's *A Room of One's Own*, Margaret Atwood's *The Handmaid's Tale*, and Simone de Beauvoir's *The Second Sex*. Her cozy little kitchen would always smell like bacon and cheese, but she would love it regardless. She would have a place to call home. She would have a nice bed, not extravagant but comfortable. She would lie in it at night and recall all those nights spent sleeping in the street, at the mercy of Mother Luck. She would be safe in her comfortable bed, safe with her little library and her little garden. And someday, she would have a boyfriend, a decent guy. Not necessarily a cute guy, though—cute guys are usually untrustworthy—a quiet guy, a respectful guy who would work hard and come home dirty. Hope amused herself with her thoughts. She daydreamed about this utopic little house for hours every day. She tried her best to avoid Harry. She did not want him to see the gleaming light of hope that had enlightened her life. Her only ally was the element of surprise. She usually waited until he left for work to get up and walk around the house; she rushed back to her room every night as soon as Harry pulled up into the driveway.

That Friday night, she sat on the couch and waited for Harry to get home. Harry never showed up. It was a beautiful Friday night, a night just like the night of their first date. *Harry is out there skimming for his next victim*, she thought. He was probably at the Concord, selling broken dreams to some naive girl. Or maybe he was out drinking with his filthy-rich doctor friends, saying filthy things about the women they lay with at night after their wives turned them down because of their filthy liquor-stinking breath. Hope did not feel an ounce of jealousy as she imagined all the things Harry could be doing on this beautiful Friday night. She eventually fell asleep on the couch.

The high-beam lights of Harry's car woke her up at around 1:45 a.m. She jumped off the couch and ran up the stairs. She stubbed her pinky toe on the edge of a table as she rushed down the hallway. She clenched her teeth, muffled her screech, and hopped on one leg to the bedroom. She slid under her bedcover and placed the pillow over her head. Hope braced herself for the nightly insults, warnings, and empty threats. As the common Haitian saying goes, *If you live with a pig long enough, you become familiar with its grunting and squealing.* Harry had become predictable in his lowly behavior. That night, however, Hope waited in vain for Harry to shout insults from the first floor. She heard Harry's almost indiscernible footsteps tiptoeing up the stairs. It was as if he was trying not to wake her up. He approached her door. Hope grabbed onto the bedsheet and wished him away. Harry opened up the bedroom door slowly and ogled Hope on the bed. Hope closed her eyes tightly; her labored breathing almost betrayed her semblance of somnolence. *Go away, go away, go away,* she thought to herself. Thankfully, Harry closed the door back up and went into the guest room. Hope was happily confused by Harry's sudden change of behavior. She got up quietly, locked her door from the inside, and went back to bed. It did not take her long to fall into a deep slumber; the rush of adrenaline had drained her of her energy.

She woke up late the following morning. She looked through the window as usual to check and see if Harry had left for tennis practice. To her great surprise, both of Harry's cars were sitting in the garage. Hope heard the TV playing louder than usual. From the second-floor hallway, she saw Harry slouching on the couch with a half-empty glass of orange juice in one hand and the TV remote in the other. Harry was not watching the sports channel as usual; he was watching the news channel. Hope thought about going downstairs to get some breakfast but opted against it. She turned around and began to walk back to her room, but the newscaster's voice caught her attention.

"Late last night, the fire department was called in for a fire raging through the bushes under Rhapsodic Bridge. The authorities had to stop all traffic, causing major delays to both southbound and northbound traffic. The fire department was able to contain the fire and limit damage to the bridge. Unfortunately, there was one fatality. The fire claimed the life of an unidentified female who has apparently been living under the bridge for years, according to officials. Her body was found in what firefighters referred to as the heart of the fire. She was burned beyond recognition, but according to the medical examiner, she was in her late thirties. The cause of the fire has not been officially determined yet. An inside source told us that the young lady may have been smoking inside of the tent made of cardboard boxes. She apparently fell asleep, forgetting to put out her cigarette. The fire marshal also found a couple of bottles of whisky that unfortunately served as accelerant to the fire. It is an unfortunate incident that, once again, sheds some light on the homelessness issue this city is facing. Our deepest condolences go to the family of the deceased woman."

"Oh God. Oh God. No!" screamed Hope. "She does not smoke. She does not drink. You killed her. Didn't you? You murdering son of a whore. You killed her." She ran downstairs and fearlessly launched a shower of punches at Harry.

"You killed her! You found out she was helping me, and you killed her. I know you did it. I know you did it, you bastard!" she screamed as she kept coming at him.

Harry backed away to avoid her punches; he was caught off guard by her reaction. He must not have known that she was watching the news. Or maybe he did. Maybe he wanted her to know that all hope was gone. Hope launched at him again and again, swinging, kicking, and screaming. She backed him into a corner. She grabbed a large wooden vase and charged at him.

After getting hit many times, Harry finally held her by her arms and restricted her movement. "Enough!" he yelled as he pushed her away. Hope tripped over the glass table and fell on the floor, hitting her head against the edge of the coffee table. She tried to get up immediately. She held onto the sofa, but she slipped in her own blood and fell back down on the floor. She was bleeding profusely from a laceration to her forehead. She tried to get up a second time, but her legs were too wobbly.

"You are a fucking murderer! You killed her because she was helping me leave your sorry ass!" she continued to scream while on the floor.

"Shut your mouth! You try to divorce me? You try to leave me? You can never leave me, at least not alive." Harry screamed as he kicked her repeatedly while she was down. Her collarbone sustained multiple blows from an enraged Harry. She raised her arms to cover her head and neck, but he proceeded to kick her in her stomach and rib cage.

Hope suffered a concussion. She woke up in her bed with a bandage around her head. There was a sour, metallic taste in her mouth. Her swollen, busted lips hurt like hell. She tried to turn around, but a sharp, excruciating pain shot through her entire body. She had several bruised and broken ribs that needed immediate attention. Yet Harry did not bother taking her to a hospital. Every bone, every muscle in her body was hurting, yet all that physical pain was nothing compared to the razor-sharp ache ripping through her chest. She had lost her best friend, her older sister, her everything.

Hope started to put the dots together. Harry had known where Catherine lived because he once followed Hope home. He must have found out that Catherine came to visit Hope, and he must have had her followed. That was the only way he could have known what Catherine was up to. Hope now understood why Harry had come home so late the night before and why he had checked on her to see if she was asleep.

All hope was lost. There would not be any divorce, there would not be a little house in the countryside, and there would be no more Catherine. Hope was inconsolable. She was responsible for Catherine's death, and that was a guilt she would have to carry with her until her last days. She had once walked the very dark path of suicide, and she had made a promise to herself to never again take the easy way out. It was a promise that she was now considering breaking. What was she supposed to do now? How was she going to live with herself, knowing that her best friend paid the ultimate cost for trying to help her?

Hope grabbed the phone frantically and dialed 911. She froze as the operator picked up. She opened her mouth, but it seemed as if her vocal cords had stopped working; not one sound came out. Hope panicked and hung up the phone. She wanted to tell the police that Harry had killed Catherine, but she did not have any proof. It was her word against Harry's. Who was going to believe her? Who was going to take her word over Harry's word? She was a housewife on the verge of a mental breakdown. Harry was a powerful man who had built a respectable reputation. It would take more than empty accusations to tie him to the Rhapsodic Bridge fire. He had no apparent tie with Catherine. Catherine was nobody. She had no family and no last name. Nobody besides Hope was going to miss her.

Hope barely left her bed for two weeks. Her room was starting to get cluttered again. Her skin was pale and soft. She developed many blisters on her back from staying in bed too long. Her recurring headaches and dizziness kept her in bed all day long sometimes. Every time she sneezed or coughed, a sharp pain on her left side reminded her of her broken ribs. She barely saw Harry. He hired a maid to watch her. The maid was more like a warden. She was at every corner Hope turned, advising Hope to return to bed.

 "You are still suffering from your head injury. It is best if you stay in bed," she said.

It was clear to Hope that the maid was much more than a maid to Harry. She walked around the house as though she owned the place. She slept in the guest room at times, undoubtedly sharing Harry's bed while Hope languished in pain upstairs.

CHAPTER XIX

***

Hope was so overwhelmed with emotions that it numbed her brain. She cared very little about Harry's housemaid prancing around the house. She cared very little about everything, including herself. She woke up every morning just to relive the loss of Catherine. Why? Why did it have to be Catherine? Why did Hope not see it coming? She slowly succumbed to the weight of the guilt she carried. She watched powerlessly as sadness created havoc within her mind. How could one understand the depth of death? The passing of a loved one leaves a void that can only be filled with sorrow and regrets. Hope blamed herself again and again. *I should have stopped her. I shouldn't have let her get involved,* she thought to herself. She spent hours scrolling through her phone, looking at pictures of Catherine, trying to make sense of the tragedy that shook the very foundation of her world.

Meanwhile, Harry's incommensurable professional success had kept him away from the house. He opened his personal clinic downtown. He worked long hours at the Ashbourne Valley Medical Center on Mondays, Wednesdays, and Fridays. He worked at his private clinic on Tuesdays and Thursdays. His busy schedule kept him in town for days at times, so he leased a flat in the business district to rest up after work. Hope found solace in the fact that she rarely crossed path with Harry.

That Tuesday morning, Harry arrived at work in a cheery mood. He was always in a cheery mood whenever there were women around. Everyone knew he was married, and everyone praised him for his kind heart. They found it noble that he allowed love to prevail regardless of Hope's social status. He kept a framed wedding picture on his desk at all times to keep the lie alive. He needed to maintain this illusion of a happy home, which had earned him so much respect around the clinic. Some of the nurses even envied Hope. If only they'd known the kind of hell Hope lived in.

Harry was well aware that more than half of the women at the clinic were interested in him. He knew of their admiration, and he knew of their desire to lose themselves in his arms. It made him feel relevant, important. Yet he never mustered the strength to approach any of these women. How could he? He was just too weak and scared to approach anyone he perceived as strong-minded. He was too weak to approach anyone that could challenge his core misogynistic beliefs.

Harry had just sat at his desk when someone knocked lightly on his office's door.

"Yes. Who is it?" yelled Harry from his desk.
"It's me, Mr. Huntelaard," replied his secretary.
"Just come on in, Gabrielle. How many times do I have to tell you this door is never locked for you?" replied Harry with a smile.

Gabrielle was a Yale graduate student who worked part time at the clinic to pay for her tuition. She was about five foot six. Her caramel skin and long curly hair contributed to her exotic looks. Harry was fond of her. Her perfume was unique, noticeable yet delicate. Her voice, although suave and sensual, had a certain seriousness to it. She was always professionally dressed, but there was a natural hint of seduction in the way she carried herself. She was not the most beautiful woman at the clinic, but she surely was the most imposing and intriguing one. At only twenty-three years of age, she was quite possibly the most intelligent one as well. She mastered in biochemistry and quantum physics. Melodiousness rolled over her tongue and out of her mouth whenever she spoke. Her eloquence equaled her elegance.

"This envelope arrived for you this morning via certified mail, sir. I signed for it as you requested," she said as she walked toward Harry's desk and handed him a medium-sized dark-brown envelope.

"Thank you, dear. They are Super Bowl tickets that I ordered last week. Premium seats too, courtside! You should come with," said Harry as he grabbed the envelope from Gabrielle and placed it on his desk.

"I wish I could, sir. I will be out of town. Maybe next year!" said Gabrielle.

"Oh, come on! What plans could you possibly have that supersede field side eats at the Super Bowl? And free booze!"

"I will be with family, sir. I would have definitely come if I did not have a prior engagement. Sorry."

Gabrielle walked out immediately to avoid any awkward conversation. She was among the very few women at the clinic who were not under Harry's spell. She had seen right through him the day she got hired, and she had been keeping her distance since.

Harry spent his morning and early afternoon completing charts and calling patients. He would have kept working if not for his growling stomach reminding him that it was way past lunchtime. He was in the mood for some sushi and decided to go for a short drive down Main Street to his favorite sushi bar. As he grabbed his car keys, the dark-brown envelope

235

stood out among other scattered papers on his desk. He was certain that they were his super bowl tickets.

Harry ripped the envelope open and pulled out an eight-page booklet. His arm muscles immediately tensed up. He paced back and forth as if he were trapped inside of his office like a caged bird. His sweaty palms dampened the corner of the booklet; balls of sweat formed on his forehead and nose and trickled down alongside his temple. Anger slowly siphoned oxygen out of his lungs. He cracked open a window in his seventeenth-floor office. A gush of fresh air rushed in and offered a semblance of solace to his labored breathing. He clenched his fist, bared his teeth, and continued pacing back and forth from his desk to the window. The more he looked at the letter, the faster his pacing got. He was being consumed from within. As he began talking to himself fairly loudly, an ensemble of nurses gathered behind his locked door, perplexed and curious, worried even. They had never seen him angry before; his acrimonious behavior was cause for concern. None of the nurses dared to knock on his door to check on him. They all looked at Gabrielle. They did not utter a word, but their worried faces called on Gabrielle to go check on the doctor. She took a deep breath and slowly opened the door. She was stunned by Harry, screaming his lungs out.

"Fucking bitch!" he shouted as he threw the wedding picture that sat on his desk against the wall. Gabrielle backed out of the room quietly and closed the door back up. The picture frame shattered beyond repair into many small pieces, thus sharing the fate of Harry's marriage. A gust of wind scooped up the wedding picture and took it out of the window. Harry tried to catch it, but it was too late. The picture was free at last—free of constraint, free to fly away and land wherever it pleased. Harry helplessly looked at the picture flying away, dancing to the cadence of the wind. He looked at the picture rising up in the sky until it disappeared into the clouds.

Harry stared broodingly at the divorce papers. In them, he saw Hope breaking free. In them, he saw Hope growing wings and flying into the unknown. Harry was not going to let that happen. He ripped up the divorce papers and calmly discarded them through the window. He watched as the wind dispersed the pieces in different directions. He walked to his closet, grabbed a bottle of whisky, and poured himself a glass. He drank it all in one shot. It was almost as if the whisky had spoken to him. He decisively snatched his keys off the table and walked out of the office with his bottle of whisky. The nurses avoided making eye contact with him as he coasted through the clinic and into the elevator.

Harry arrived home right before nightfall. He was very much inebriated. He pushed the double doors open and came face to face with the housemaid he had hired to watch over Hope. "Go home," he said to her in a neutral, passive voice. She walked out of the house immediately, and Harry locked the doors behind her. He stood in the middle of the living room for an instant, looking around in silence as if he was trying to decide his next course of action. He began to whistle an old tune, "In the Hall of the Mountain King." He whistled nonchalantly as he walked up the stairs and made his way to the bathroom. He removed his tie and suit and threw them on the floor. He then turned on the water to fill up the bathtub, whistling away still. The old, creepy tune intensified with every step Harry took toward Hope's bedroom. The whistling suddenly stopped. Hope waited anxiously for Harry to walk away.

Harry kicked the door open and stumbled inside of the bedroom. He yanked Hope by her hair and dragged her off the bed. Hope started kicking and yelling, grabbing onto everything and anything around her. Harry tightened his grip to make sure she didn't wiggle away. As he dragged Hope down the hallway, a river of blood oozed alongside her temple. Chunks of hair ripped off her scalp each time Harry took a step and dragged her behind him. She screamed… and screamed again. Her quavering voice grew weaker and weaker. She grabbed onto Harry's left foot and supplicated him to stop. "Stop, Harry, please stop," she said in an undertone. Harry lodged a mild kick between her neck and shoulder, knocking the wind out of her. He dragged her all the way to the bathroom, indifferent to the trail of blood and bloody hair he had left behind, indifferent to Hope's supplications. He dropped onto his knees and grabbed her by the neck with his free hand. He then shoved her head into the already-overflowing tub.

The bubbling crimson water splashed all over the floor. Harry watched her twitching and twisting. He watched Hope battling to hold onto life. Her frantic hands began to shake. Her muscles began to ache. Her chest tightened as water replaced the air in her lungs. The shimmering lights of the bathroom rippling against the surface of the water began to fade away. She tried to push herself up, in the direction of the light, but the numbness in her legs left her helpless. As the last breath of life appeared to be leaving her body, Harry laughed maniacally and pulled her up. Air rushed into her lungs, causing her to breathe shallowly. She spluttered then opened her eyes. Her dilated pupils appeared to be bleeding from within. If there was anything more frightening than dying, it was almost dying. Hope almost died. Her skin was translucent; her arms, shaky; her gaze, doleful. Fear was etched on her face like a gypsy curse carved on precious stones.

"Divorce papers? Served to me at my workplace? You still try to divorce me, ungrateful piece of shit?" said Harry in a raucous voice. "And you thought I was going to just let you walk away."

Hope looked puzzled. *Divorce papers? What divorce papers?* Even after her death, Catherine was helping her. Catherine must have filed for divorce on behalf of Hope before the fire.

Before Hope could make sense of it all, Harry plunged her head into the water again as she tried to speak. She gasped for air and attempted to scream, but water gushed into her mouth. Harry spent nearly an hour toying with Hope. He toyed with her life over and over, ceaselessly plunging her into the water and pulling her out right before the last light of life left her body. Hope had lost so much blood from her scalp that she was falling in and out of consciousness. She blurted out senseless words every time she emerged from the bathtub. Eventually, she became completely idle—unresponsive. Harry pulled her out and dragged her back to bed after doing CPR to revive her. She no longer had hair on her head for Harry to grip, so he snatched the collar of her shirt and pulled her up into her bedroom. Harry threw her inert body on the bed and locked the door from the outside. Hope grabbed the nearest pillow and hugged it tightly. Curled up in the fetal position, she lay there with her eyes wide open, gazing at the wall with a blank stare. She dozed off a few hours later.

The following morning, Harry canceled all his plans and stayed home. It was a beautiful, quiet Wednesday morning. The sun rose from the east, as it always does. The blackbirds sang their morning tunes as usual until a couple of feral cats chased them away, as usual. The first shimmer of sun entered Hope's window and cuddled her face while she was asleep, as usual.

She slowly opened her eyes; she grunted as she got off the bed. She staggered her way to the mirror to assess the damage caused by her beloved husband. She was beyond recognition. She had large random bald spots on her scalp. The little hair she had left was all red and tangled. It was as if bees had feasted on her swollen cheeks; the gash on her forehead had reopened. Two of her front teeth had vanished, and she had more bruises than she could count.

Hope showed no emotion as she examined her face then her body. She showed a stupendous display of strength in the face of adversity. What she lacked in physical strength, she made up for in strength of character. Catherine would have wanted her to be strong. She walked back to the bed, removed the wet sheets, and threw them on the floor. Using scissors lying on the dresser, she cut off the little bit of hair

241

left. She struggled to hold the scissors due to excruciating pain from her broken collarbone. She used peroxide and ginger ale to clean up her scalp. She was too hurt from within to feel the sting of the ginger ale touching her scalp. She then wrapped her head up with a soft cotton headwrap and went back to bed.

Hope was no longer that delicate flower waiting to bloom. The verbal abuse had taken away her dignity, and the physical abuse had taken away her sanity and her beauty. She should have walked away at the first sign of disrespect. She should have walked away at the first sign of abuse. Instead, she stayed for the sake of love. She lived to love; love was her downfall. She wished to cry and release the ruefulness bearing down on her chest. She hoped to sob a little—just so she could have that sense of relief that usually followed. Her well of tears had run dry.

She stayed in bed all day long until the late afternoon. At around five o'clock, Harry walked into the room with a plate of lobster, pickles, and sirloin steak. He stumbled over a towel on the floor but miraculously managed to hold onto the plate. The fork and the steak knife fell under the bed.
"Well, seems like you are going to have to eat with your hands, my sweet. Come here. Share this steak with me," he joked. "Look at your face! Look what you made me do to you!"

Hope never took her eyes off the ceiling. It was as if Harry were a ghost, a mere figment of her imagination. She knew he would eventually get upset; she wanted him to get upset. She wanted him to end the madness he had started. Her only way out of this misery was death, but she was not going to make it easy for Harry. She wanted her blood on Harry's hands. If Harry wanted her dead, he would have to do it himself. She stared at the ceiling and silently begged him to unleash his rage on her one last time.

"You are going to get me upset, Hope. I am talking to you! You do not want me to get upset," warned Harry. His voice sounded so distant to Hope. She wanted to scream at him. She wanted to tell him that he was sick, mentally exhausting, and sociopathic. She did no such thing. She let him rant and make elaborate threats.

After various attempts to get a reaction out of Hope, Harry threw the plate of food onto the floor and dragged Hope off the bed by her feet. Her head hit the ground so hard that it resonated throughout the entire house. Hope did not emit a single sound—not a scream, not a word, not a grunt! Harry climbed on top of her and started choking her with his bare hands. She smiled and spread her arms out in defeat.

"You are my wife, aren't you? Tell me, when was the last time I had you? You don't remember? Well, today is our lucky day, it seems. Let me remind you what I feel like," said Harry as he ripped her brassiere off open and shoved his hand under her dress.

These words reverberated inside of Hope's head like bullets ricocheting over and over. She was not afraid of dying. She was already dead inside. Yet she could never tolerate the thought of another man entering her temple against her will. She refused to relive her worst nightmare. Harry continued to grope her breast and thighs while pinning her down with one hand. She felt his penis harden up against her thighs. The stench of whisky on Harry's breath slapped her on the face as he leaned over to get a grip on her underwear. Harry ripped off her panties in a single motion as she twisted and turned to keep her legs closed.

"No. I will fucking kill you, Harry, you sick bastard. Stop. I swear I will fucking kill you!" she screamed. He spat on her face twice and shoved a pair of sandals in her mouth to keep her from screaming. He let go of Hope's hands momentarily and began to unbutton his pants. It was happening. She was about to re-experience the most traumatic moment of her life at the hand of the husband she used to love. In a herculean outburst of courage, Hope managed to slightly push Harry off her.

It is said that "when the vital nerve is severed, the chicken kills the wildcat." The vital nerve had been severed. Hope was consumed by the fear of being raped a second time—her biggest fear—a fear that surpassed the fear of death itself. Blood sailed from her racing heart and through her veins at the speed of light. She felt rage boiling inside of her, begging to get out, begging to be set free. She succumbed to the supplications of her inner beast. She set her rage free. Before Harry realized what was happening, Hope pulled a drawer out of the dresser and hit him in the face. He stumbled onto his knees. Droplets of blood leaked from his face as he tried to get up. A stream of blood started rolling down his cheeks from the laceration above his left eye. He held onto the bed to get up but pulled the sheet off and fell right back on the floor. In the meantime, Hope had gotten a hold of the steak knife. She climbed on top of him, holding the steak knife under his throat.

"Think about what you are doing. You will go to prison for the rest of your life," begged Harry in the midst of desperation. His lips became dry and his voice, crackly and choky. The begging suddenly stopped; Harry gagged on his own words.

The cold, sharp knife sliced though his neck with the ease of a samurai sword cutting through butter. As Hope pulled out the knife, blood sprinkled all over her face from the gaping hole in Harry's neck. She wiped her eyes clear and looked at Harry with disdain. There was a hint of satisfaction mixed with anger in her eyes. "You fucking pig!" she screamed as she stabbed Harry again and again. Blood splattered all over the floor. Hope sat on top of him like a conqueror on his horse, staring down a defeated enemy. She was possessed by the gods of retribution, brandishing the bloody knife and stabbing nonstop. "Die! Just die!" she screamed repeatedly. Her facial expression grew more satisfied every time the knife entered Harry's chest. With every thrust came that satisfying slushing sound that motivated Hope even more.

Harry lay on the floor, powerless, swimming in a pool of his own blood. He tried to scream, but the cavernous hole in his throat was spewing out blood like a fountain of good fortune on Sunday morning.

"Die! Die! Die!" she yelled. She looked at him twitching and bleeding. She paused for an instant; she paused to enjoy sweet memories of Catherine's goofiness that came rushing in. She paused for an instant, but his repugnantly handsome face and perfect cheeks made her uneasy. She carved her uneasiness on his face. The slashing continued until Harry was completely disfigured.

Hope suddenly dropped the knife and held her head with both hands. A sharp, stabbing pain radiated around her forehead; electrical waves traveled through her brain. Memories flooded her mind like ripples on a lake—overwhelming memories. The shock of the gruesome stabbing triggered something unexplainable inside of her head. Buried memories of her past life rushed in. It was like an anamnesis, a scary recollection of a previous life. Like a space traveler trapped between two worlds, Hope struggled to rearrange the influx of memories flooding her mind. At first, it felt as if it were all the fruit of her imagination. Hope thought she was losing her mind. She thought she was making it all up in her head to escape the gruesome reality she was sitting on top of. Yet as the pain started to fade away, her recollections became clearer and clearer. She was not losing her mind. She had actual memories of her life before the desert—memories as clear as day.

She remembered everything. She remembered her name, her real name: Rosellys Malloy. She saw her son's deep-brown eyes gazing at her sadly every morning before she left for work. And her cat, Malice, always so friendly, was always on her lap when she read or took a nap. She remembered her fiancé— the sweetest man Earth had ever produced. She remembered her engagement party—the extravagance, the abundance of guests, the excitement. Then she remembered Dee—Delilah Walters, the host of her engagement party.

Publisher's Afterword

***

Relevance

Life is a complex kaleidoscope. We are all complicated beings and we are all driven by a desire for supremacy. It is intrinsically human to want to feel superior. However, we ought to repress that innate tendency to compete and strive for mutual respect and equality. *The Illusions of Hope* only scratches the surface of human's complexity.

Who am I? The Identity Dilemma

Who am I? We rarely ask ourselves such question. Yet, our entire existence seems to be driven by the need to find our true purpose. *The Illusions of Hope* is the tale of a woman's quest for the meaning of life – a woman's quest for identity and purpose. Hope's journey is one of self-discovery; it is tumultuous and challenging. The struggles she went through contributed to the shaping of her personality. Despite her misfortunes, she emerged as the symbol of resilience, strength and perseverance. It is highly anticipated that the author will bring her back as a highly empowered and purpose-driven character in the second installment of the *Hope series*.

The author made the bold choice to be unapologetically graphic when describing both horrific and exhilarating moments of Hope's journey. When asked about his decision to be so direct, he stated that *"It was a decision made based on the fact that life itself does not sugarcoat anything. Life is raw and anything that is life-related should be delivered in its purest, raw form."* Although some passages may have unsettled the readers, we cannot deny that life itself unsettles us more often than not. The author delivered a gut-wrenching tale that will surely spark both pleasant and unpleasant conversations.

Style and language.

The language of *The Illusions of Hope* is fluid; Auguste's prose gives life to the story being told. Auguste is a poet before anything else and his style surely reflects that. His written works have been influenced by French poets from the romanticism era (Victor Hugo, Alfred de Vigny, Alphonse de Lamartine). Auguste has always embraced the notion that the world is asymmetrical. The world is a chaotic delight. He embraces the belief that the mind should be able to wander freely without any constraint. The poet should be freed from the constraint of forms and rhymes. The only expectation and requirement should be the musicality of touching words.

Auguste's style has also been deeply influenced by the surrealist movement (Paul Eluard, Louis Aragon) and the exploration of the mind beyond what is known and understood.

Auguste's debut novel offers a glimpse into his versatility. It is to be noted that the dramatic ending of *The Illusions of Hope* hints at a sequel. According to Auguste, this book is the first installment in the *Hope series*. We, at Sentinel Creations Press, do hope to see more of Auguste's fast-paced, fluid story telling ability in the future.

Sentinel Creations Press,
April 15, 2018